PROLOGUE

Connor McBride let out a frustrated sigh.

Exactly one month before, a blue-eyed, dark-haired beauty had waltzed into his tavern, swung her leg over the bar stool, and crooked her finger at him. He'd felt like a sailor being lured against the rocks by a sultry siren. Taking her order, he'd wanted to drop his elbows on the bar, gaze into her sweet, sassy eyes, and maybe, if the Gods were willing, get her phone number.

She had mesmerized him.

Sapphire eyes framed by dark lashes had sparkled up at him, and her dark hair falling around her shoulders begged to be clutched as he tasted her pink luscious lips. When he'd handed her a beer, she'd ignored the glass, and placing the nozzle to her mouth, she tilted back her head and drank several swallows before pulling it away and breaking into a grin. It had been so damn sexy he'd wanted to lean over the bar, rip it out of her hands, and crush her mouth like it was his last night on earth.

But five minutes was all he'd had.

That night his bar had been busy.

Crazy busy.

The Friday after Thanksgiving, the regulars would join together and celebrate the holidays. The ritual had started years before when he'd held an Eggnog and Christmas Tree Decorating Happy Hour. On offer was a free punchbowl of whiskey-laced eggnog, plenty of tasty munchies, and shiny baubles for the freshly chopped tree. The event had been a huge success, and the business had blossomed. McBride's Bar and Grill became the place to hang out, and the annual Christmas tree decorating night had turned into a ritual.

Called to serve another customer, he'd hurried away, but when he'd turned to shoot her a smile, she'd left. The empty beer bottle sat on the counter looking abandoned and forlorn, as if it too, was wishing she'd come back and wrap her painted nails around its barrel.

He'd spent days asking around, but no-one knew her.

She was a mystery woman.

Every night since, he'd prayed for her return.

As the days turned into weeks, and she failed to appear, he almost became resigned to the idea she wouldn't be back and he'd just have to accept it.

Almost.

Glancing up at the antique wagon-wheel clock above the door, another sigh left his lips. It was well past closing time. He'd fallen into the habit of leaving the door unlocked as he finished cleaning up, hoping she'd drop by for a nightcap. Even though it was Christmas Eve, he maintained the vigil.

He'd considered flying back to the city to visit his parents and sister, but he couldn't shake the notion the gorgeous, unnamed woman would wander in during the Christmas holiday. Standing with the broom in his hand, he cursed himself for being obsessively hopeful.

"Lord, what possessed me?" he muttered. "I could be sittin' around the fire smellin' mom's cinnamon cake instead of standin' here sweepin' this damn floor."

Shaking his head, he continued his work, lifting the chairs and placing them on top of the tables as he moved around the room. But as he had done many nights before, he headed back behind the bar to play the Brad Paisley hit that haunted him as much as she did.

We Danced.

As the song began, he heard a gust of wind whistle around the building. Walking quickly to the nearest window, he peered outside. Snow swirled in the air. It would be a chilly, blustery Christmas Eve.

When he'd first bought the tavern, he'd built a cozy apartment in the abandoned storage area up a winding staircase above the kitchen. As his business grew, he'd bought a house on several acres. But he often

HER CHRISTMAS COWBOY

Maggie Carpenter

(Second Edition)

Published by

Dark Secrets Press

Cover

https://fantasiafrogdesigns.wordpress.com

Visit the author at:

https://www.Amazon.com/author/maggiecarpenter

www.MaggieCarpenter.com/blog

www.facebook.com/MaggieCarpenterWriter

stayed in his old digs, and with the winter storm kicking up, he decided to stick around. The night was dark, and the roads would be icy.

As the song came to an end, he finished sweeping, pulled the blinds down across the windows, and put away the last of the glassware. Wearily moving through the kitchen and up the stairs, he poured himself a snifter of Cognac, kicked off his boots, and flopped down on the couch. As he sipped the warm, soothing drink, his mind took him back to Cat.

The woman who had changed his life.

Cat, short for Catherine.

He'd been living in the city, and she was the personification of fun and fashion. Super-smart and equally ambitious, she knew all the trendy places to eat and drink.

But Cat had a secret.

One night, returning to his apartment after dinner, she'd crawled over his lap, and looked at him over her shoulder with pleading eyes.

"I've been a bad girl," she'd muttered. "Please will you spank me?"

Astonished but tantalized by her request, he'd smoothed his palm across her upturned backside, then landed a solid swat. She'd dropped her head, let out a low moan, then wiggled for more.

He'd delivered a second, and a third.

As he'd continued, bouncing his hand from cheek to cheek, his cock stiffened to life. When she began squealing and promising to behave, he'd raised her skirt and studied the pink stain along the sides of her french-cut panties.

Energy had surged through his loins.

Slipping a finger inside the crotch of the sexy underwear, he'd found her gloriously, deliciously wet. Sex that night had been unlike any he'd ever had, and he'd suddenly found himself catapulted into a whole new lifestyle—a lifestyle he loved.

But the hustle and bustle of urban life was like sandpaper against his soul. He longed for the mountains, clean air, room to breathe, and horses. When his relationship with Cat had run its course, he'd sold up and moved into the small rural town.

He'd yet to meet another woman who relished the kind of attention he longed to offer them. A few had acquiesced to his dark desires, but he knew they'd done so simply to please him.

They didn't *love* it.

They didn't *crave* it.

They didn't *need* it as he did.

Wishing he could share the holidays with a kindred spirit, he placed his brandy snifter on the coffee table, stretched out on the couch, closed his eyes and thought about the following day.

He'd spend it with Lance Chapman, the man who had sold him the bar. Whenever he was at Lance's ranch, Connor felt happy and fulfilled. Horses, dogs, cattle, a few goats, three crazy kids, and a warm, pretty wife who doted on her husband and their cozy home.

Lance's life was Connor's dream.

He loved spending time with them, but even as he thought about the joy he'd be fortunate to share, his mind began to wander to the dark-haired girl with the naughty blue eyes and ridiculously kissable lips. Unzipping his fly and reaching for his cock, he imagined himself behind the bar as she picked up the beer bottle, winked at him with a wicked grin, then wrapped her mouth around the nozzle and tilted it up. Closing his eyes, he let his fantasy take hold.

"You make good beer," she declared as she lowered it down, then leaning over the bar, her enticing cleavage impossible to ignore, she added, *"and I'll bet you make good other things too."*

"I haven't had any complaints."

"And what would you do if a girl were to complain—just to be difficult?"

He could hear her voice—teasing, almost mocking him.

"I'd say that girl might be in for a surprise."

"What kind of surprise?"

His vision jumped forward.

She was kneeling on the barstool, her elbows resting on the counter with her back arched as his hand swatted her naked backside. Her squeals echoed through the empty bar, and as he paused to study her crimson skin, his eyes fell on her glistening pussy.

His climax suddenly swept over him with a series of explosive spasms. His essence burst across his hand, and as it slowly sputtered to an end, he let out a heavy sigh, opened his eyes, and looked around for something to wipe himself.

"Dammit," he muttered seeing nothing in reach.

Too tired to move, he pulled off his T-shirt, cleaned himself up, dropped it on the floor, then laid back down and let out a yawn.

"Lord, I don't care how you do it, just bring her back through my door."

Closing his eyes he let himself doze, her image dancing in the fore-front of his mind the last thing he saw as he dozed off.

* * *

A loud bang startled him from sleep.

Sitting up and wiping his hands over his face, he glanced at the small glowing numbers on his DVD. 2:04 a.m.

The wind sounded furious.

A shiver pricked his skin, but not from the cold.

Breaking branches and blowing debris could cause serious damage.

Abruptly realizing he'd forgotten to lock up, he rose to his feet, and was zipping up his jeans when he heard another noise.

A startling noise.

Footsteps in the bar.

His heart thumping, he left his boots off and crept silently across the room. Opening a cabinet and carefully lifting out a metal box, he raised the lid, picked up his revolver, and hastily loaded the chamber.

Another bang.

Taking a long deep breath, he crept down the stairs, cringing when he heard a squeak. Continuing to creep through the kitchen, he reached the swinging door that led into the bar and peered through the small glass window.

He caught his breath.

A body in a full length, black puffer coat was lying in the middle of the floor.

Cracking open the door, he scanned the bar. Seeing no-one else, he stuffed the gun into the back of his jeans and hurried to the motionless figure. As he crouched down and tentatively touched an arm, the person groaned and rolled over.

"Please help me..."

His mystery woman, as pale as the moon with scrapes on her face, stared up at him.

CHAPTER ONE

Letting out a long breath, her eyes closed back down. Hoping her sorry state was from exhaustion, and not an injury or something serious, he was about to pick her up when a car's horn blasted repeatedly. Seconds later, the flash of headlights against the window shades announced the arrival of a vehicle.

His heart skipped.

Instinctively sensing danger, he darted to the door and locked the deadbolt, then raced back and scooped her up. Half-opening her eyes, she put her arms around his neck, buried her head in his chest, and clung to him as if her life depended on it.

A protective energy surged through his soul.

Carrying her up the winding staircase and into his bedroom, he laid her on the bed, removed the drenched coat, and her wet boots and socks. Her jeans and sweater appeared relatively dry, and relieved there was no evidence of blood or obvious injuries, hastily covered her with a blanket.

"P-please, w-will y-you help m-me?" she whispered through chattering teeth.

"Of course I'll help you."

A loud pounding at his door made him jump.

"Oh, G-God," she muttered, terror in her half-lidded eyes. "P-please, d-don't t-ell them I'm h-here."

"Don't worry. I'll send them on their way," he promised, smoothing rogue tendrils of wet hair from her face. "You stay here and get warm. I'll be right back."

Hurrying from the room, he trotted quickly down the stairs. Though reassured by the gun pressing against the small of his back, he fervently prayed he wouldn't have to use it. As he marched through the kitchen, the urgent pounding started again. Continuing through the tavern to the door, he didn't respond right away, but took a few seconds to compose himself.

"Who is it?"

"Sorry to bother you," a man's voice called back. "Would you please let us in? It's freezing out here."

The word *us,* caught Connor's attention.

"You got me outta bed. Whatta ya need? I can call someone for you, but I'm not openin' the door."

He held his breath.

Whoever they were, they sounded frantic, and there was nothing to stop them smashing in the windows.

"Have you seen a dark-haired girl in the last hour or so?" the man shouted. "She's mentally unstable and we need to find her. She proba-bly would've asked to use your phone."

A chill rattled through his body.

He didn't believe the accusation for a moment.

"I've been closed for hours, and if it's all the same to you I'd like to go back to bed."

"Okay. Sorry to have bothered you."

Hearing the tromp of feet as the men trudged away, he moved swiftly to the closest window and peered through a crack in the closed blinds. Two men climbed into a late model Range Rover. Though he tried to read the license plate, he could only make out the last four let-ters. HILL.

They rang a bell.

Waiting until the SUV had left the parking lot and was driving away, he hurried back up the stairs and into the living room. Quickly returning his gun to its box and placing it in the cabinet, he poured a generous amount of Cognac into the brandy snifter and carried it into his bedroom. His beautiful mystery woman wasn't trembling as much, and her eyes were open.

"They're gone," he assured her, sitting on the edge of the bed. "I've brought you some brandy. It will help warm you up."

"Thank you," she mumbled, "I'm very grateful."

"That was a decent coat you were wearing," he remarked, placing the glass on the nightstand as he helped her sit up, "but not enough for this weather. Were you in the storm for very long?"

"Uh-huh, I guess. It sure felt like it."

"Here, drink this," he said, offering her the snifter.

Taking the glass with shaky fingers, she brought it to her lips, took a sip, let out a sigh, then took another.

"I'm Connor McBride, by the way."

"April Sullivan," she mumbled. "Thank goodness you were home."

"Nice to meet you, April," he said as she took another swallow. "I don't live here, I just stay here occasionally. April, I know it's late, but perhaps you should take a hot shower."

"Really? Thank you. That would be amazing," she stammered. "I feel like a block of ice."

"I'll just be a minute."

Stepping into the bathroom, he turned on the faucets, then moved back to the bedroom and opened the bottom drawer of his dresser. Lifting out fleecy pajamas he'd never worn, a smile crossed his lips. They'd been a gift from his mother two years before. Grateful he'd kept them, he added a pair of thick woolly socks, and laid them on the bed.

"They'll be much too big, but at least they'll be warm. You can sleep in here, I'll take the couch in the other room. The water takes a minute to get hot, but it should be okay by the time you go in."

"Thank you so much. You have no idea..." But her voice trailed off.

"You've obviously been through a helluva night, but you can tell me all about it in the morning. You need to get some sleep."

"It's Christmas t-tomorrow. You must have plans."

"April, don't worry about anything except taking that hot shower and curling into bed. I'll be back in a few minutes with a mug of my famous cocoa."

Her blue eyes looked up at him, brimming with tears and full of gratitude. Giving her hand a reassuring squeeze, he rose to his feet and walked from the room, closing the door behind him.

"I feel like I'm living in a movie," he muttered as he made his way down the stairs. "What the hell happened to her, and who were those guys?"

Turning on the kitchen lights, he placed a small saucepan on the stove, then poured in a cup of whole milk and two teaspoons of cocoa. Stirring slowly, he allowed the mixture to simmer until the cocoa was fully blended, then tipped it into a mug and added a splash of Chocolate Liqueur. Turning off the lights and making his way back up the stairs, when he reached the bedroom and didn't hear the shower, he tapped on the door.

"Come in."

Stepping inside, he found her in bed with a towel wrapped around her head, and the cuffs of the pale blue pajamas shirt rolled up. She looked diminutive and vulnerable, but the color had returned to her cheeks.

"You're so kind," she murmured, her large blue eyes staring up at him. "I don't know what I would have done if your door hadn't been open."

"It must have been fate. I still can't believe I forgot to lock it," he said, handing her the mug, marveling at her return even if it was under bizarre circumstances.

A frown suddenly crossed her brow.

"What is it, April?"

"I dropped my purse. It was so dark and cold, and I was in such a hurry, I couldn't stop to search for it."

"You poor thing," he said softly, gazing at her crinkled face as she re-lived her perilous journey. "I don't know if we'll have any luck finding it with all the snow, but I'm happy to give it a try when the storm passes. Right now you just get some rest, and try not to worry."

"I'll never be able to thank you enough for what you've done for me tonight."

"Hey, I'm just glad I was here. Drink your cocoa and get some sleep."

Rising to his feet and moving to his closet, he pulled out his extra pillow and a couple of blankets, then shooting her a warm smile, he moved into the living room. As he pulled off his jeans, he spotted his T-shirt still lying on the floor. He'd been so caught up in the drama of her arrival, he hadn't realized he'd been running around half naked.

"I really am losin' my mind," he mumbled, stretching out on the couch and flapping the blankets over him.

Sinking into the soft cushions, he was overcome by a long yawn, but as he was about to turn off the lamp on the side table there was a soft knock on the door.

"May I speak to you a minute?"

Her voice was soft, almost childlike.

He flashed back to the night he'd met her.

She was nothing like the sharp, sassy girl, driving him crazy with her kiss-me-now lips and sultry stare.

"Of course, come on in."

Wearing only the oversized socks, and the pajama shirt falling to just above her knees, she looked as sexy as hell. He had to force his eyes from the full, evident swell of her breasts, and her sharp nipples press-ing against the fleecy fabric.

"I'm sorry to bother you," she said quietly, standing in the doorway.

"Trust me, you're not botherin' me, not one bit," he replied, sitting up.

"That cocoa was delicious."

"Glad you liked it. Come on in. You don't need to hover by the door."

She stepped tentatively forward.

"It's just, uh...," she said hesitantly. "I don't want to cause you any trouble. I'll get out of your hair as soon as I wake up."

"That doesn't sound like a very good idea, and certainly not something to discuss right now. Go on back to bed. You need to rest."

"But you don't understand. Those men, if they come back..."

"If they come back, they'll find a closed sign on the door."

"If you're sure..." she stammered, "except, they're mean. Really mean."

"I can handle mean," he said with a grin. "Please, April, go back to bed and stop worrying. I won't let anything happen to you. I promise."

"Thanks again, Connor. Really. Thanks."

He watched her step backwards and close the door, but not before he spied a bright red blush cross her face.

"Damn, you're about as cute as a girl could be," he muttered, reaching behind his head and turning out the lamp.

But as he settled back down, the mystery of her dramatic appearance, and the arrival of the men looking for her, sent a dark, worried frown across his forehead.

She was scared.

Really scared.

The license plate popped to the forefront of his mind.

HILL

He was sure he knew it, but he didn't know why.

Trusting the answer would come, he listened to the fury of the storm swirling outside, and imagined her lying between his sheets.

The image sent a unique comfort through his being.

It was as if she belonged there.

It was similar to the way he felt at Lance's ranch. He was at home around the horses and livestock. His sister used to tell him he must have been a cowboy in another life. He almost believed it. He loved his bar, but he was determined to own a horse farm, and even though he barely knew her, he hoped his beautiful mystery girl would be at his side.

CHAPTER TWO

In spite of the late night drama and raging storm, Connor slept a deep, dreamless sleep. Waking to silence, he slipped off the couch and peered out the small window. The sky was grey, but there was no wind, and it had stopped snowing. Relieved and reaching for his phone, he called his family to wish them a Merry Christmas. Though he missed them, he was glad he'd listened to his instincts. He was horrified to think what might have happened to April if he hadn't been there. Finishing the call and quickly dressing, he moved from the living room to the bedroom door and gently knocked.

He wasn't surprised at the lack of response. The poor girl had been wiped out. Leaving her to sleep, he trotted down the stairs and into the kitchen. Deciding on serving her French Toast when she appeared, he broke several eggs in a bowl, added cinnamon and milk, and cut thick slices of the raisin bread he bought at the local farmers market.

With everything ready, he thought about the day ahead. He was due at Lance's around two-o'clock, but he wasn't about to leave April by herself. Pulling his phone from his pocket, he called his friend.

"Hey, Connor, Merry Christmas," Lance said cheerily. "I take it you survived the storm. Did you stay at the tavern?"

"Yep, and I'm glad, but I'll tell you why in a minute. How is everyone?"

"The kids are runnin' around like banshees and beggin' us to let them open their presents. You know we wait until after our dinner at this house."

"Such child abuse," Connor exclaimed. "Better make sure they're kept away from the phone. They'll report you."

"Actually, last night we weakened and gave them one, but kids bein' kids, give 'em an inch...!"

"I'm sure. When are you gonna tell Izzy about her pony?"

"We'll head down to the barn after dinner to give the horses their Christmas carrots,," Lance replied, dropping his voice. "The pony will be in one of the stalls."

"The other two are gonna be mighty jealous."

"Yep, but they'll get their turn. The puppy will help."

"You didn't tell me anything about a new puppy! Don't you have enough dogs around that place?"

"You'd think so, right? It was Annabelle's idea, but this one's a lapdog. The others would rather be outside chasin' rabbits than curled on up on the couch watchin' the tube. Even when the weather's bad they're runnin' in and outta the doggy door like crazy."

"A puppy and a pony. This sounds like it's gonna be a crazy Christmas," Connor remarked with a chuckle. "You're a lucky guy, Lance. You have such a great family."

"Thanks, yeah, I love 'em to bits. You still comin' over around two?"

"I am, but I had quite the night, or rather, early mornin'."

"Oh, yeah? What happened?"

"Remember my mystery girl?" he asked, lowering his voice as he walked to the foot of the stairs to make sure she wasn't on her way down.

How could I forget? You keep tellin' me she'll be back."

"She landed on my doorstep freezin' cold and about to drop. Actually, she did drop. I heard a noise, and when I came downstairs she was on the floor. I'd forgotten to lock up."

"Damn! You're kiddin' me! Is she okay?"

"I think so, but she'd been walkin' through the snowstorm. I just hope she doesn't come down with pneumonia. She took a hot shower and I let her sleep in my bed. She hasn't woken up yet, and I'm not surprised."

"You're a fast worker!"

"I wasn't with her," Connor said hastily. "I gave her those fleecy pajamas mom bought me, and made her a mug of hot chocolate."

"She sure was lucky to land on your doorstep. If there was ever a night made for your famous cocoa, last night was it."

"Yeah, for sure, but that's not all," Connor said solemnly. "A few minutes after I found her, some guys drove up in a Range Rover and banged on my door. The poor girl was scared to death. I think they'd been chasin' her."

"What the hell? Any idea who they were?"

"None, and no way was I lettin' 'em in, but when they left, I looked through the window and saw they were in a white Range Rover. I got the last four letters of their plate. H-I-L-L. Hill."

"Shit. Connor, that's not good."

"Why? What do you know?"

"That's a car from the Churchill estate. They have a fleet, and the plates are all the same, but with a number in front, like 2CCHILL, and 3CCHILL and so on."

Connor paused.

"It looked familiar," he said thoughtfully. "I guess I must have seen it around, but I'm still not sure who you're talkin' about."

"The Churchill family, the wealthy guy with five sons who lives in that huge house about thirty minutes east. He has a lotta clout around here."

"Damn," Connor muttered. "Well, I don't care who she was runnin' from, she was terrified, and she can hide out with me as long as she wants. I'll help her, whatever she needs."

"Connor, you don't wanna be messin' with them."

"I'm not messin' with anyone. I'm helpin' out a damsel in distress, and from what I saw last night she needs all the protection she can get."

"You could be the poster child for bein', lassoed at first sight."

"I wish I could argue with you, but I can't," Connor replied, letting out a heavy sigh. "You know from the moment I laid eyes on her, I was toast."

"You've got it bad."

"No shit, and I don't even know her."

"Gotta go, Annabelle's callin' me. The kids are drivin' her batty."

"Before you take off, would you mind if I brought her with me? I'm not gonna leave her alone here, especially not with those dudes after her, and it's Christmas Day."

"Sure, of course, the more the merrier. I just hope she likes mayhem."

"I guess we'll find out," Connor said with a chuckle. "I can't wait, and thanks, Lance."

"Hey, no problem, you know how Annabelle is. We'll have enough food to feed the whole damn county. One more person at the table won't even make a dent."

As he was about to make a quick comment before ending the call, Connor heard one of Lance's daughters yelling in the background. She was accusing her brother of sneaking a look at a present under the tree.

"Uh-oh, war's about to break out," Lance declared. "See you later."

"Go keep the peace," Connor replied, grinning as he imagined the scene.

Ending the call, he dropped his phone back in his pocket, poured himself a mug of coffee, and stepped outside to check his driveway. As he expected, it would have to be shoveled, but it wasn't as bad as he'd feared.

"Good morning."

April's voice, crisp and clear, came from behind him. Turning around, he saw her standing in the doorway. Though her face was freshly scrubbed without a hint of makeup, Connor thought she'd never looked more beautiful.

"Hey there, how are you feelin'?" he asked, walking up to join her. "Did you sleep well?"

"I was so tired, I could have slept through anything. Your bed is really comfortable."

"It's just a thick block of memory foam," he said, ushering her back inside. "When I was renovatin', I decided to build a platform and pick up a slab of the stuff. It worked out great. Sometimes I like it better than my regular mattress at home."

"Aren't you a clever cowboy?" she quipped with a grin, reminding him of how she'd been when they first met.

"You really do feel better. Are you hungry?"

"Starving."

"I've got everything ready to go. Breakfast will only take a few minutes."

"A clever cowboy who cooks. I'm impressed. Can I help?"

"Sure, by tellin' me what you were doin' runnin' around in that storm last night, and who showed up bangin' on my door?"

Her happy smile suddenly faded.

"Sorry, I didn't mean to upset you," he said quickly, "but you must have known I'd ask."

"Yeah, but it's a long, boring story. I'll try to make it quick. I was staying with this wealthy family, but I wanted to leave. Even though I was a bit drunk, I took off in one of their cars. I lost control on the icy road and got stuck in a ditch, but I knew they'd come after me so I couldn't hang around. Then I remembered your tavern. I thought it was just a short walk from where I'd gotten stuck, but it wasn't, it was forever. At one point I remember thinking I was walking in the wrong direction. I almost turned around. Thank goodness I didn't."

"You were probably a bit delirious," Connor murmured, imagining her terrified as she fought her way through the storm.

"Sorry for being such a nuisance."

"You're not a nuisance. Don't think that for a second," he declared, dipping the bread into the egg mixture and dropping it in the pan. "Would you like some coffee? There's plenty in the pot."

"I would love some. Thanks."

She'd told him how she'd ended up walking through the storm and searching out his bar, but she hadn't told him why she'd been determined to get away from the Churchill estate, and been so terrified of the family.

He decided not to press.

Watching her walk across the kitchen and pour herself a mug of coffee, he admired her knockout figure. As if sensing his eyes on her, she turned and smiled at him. Though he smiled back, he was unexpectedly consumed with a deep desire to take her in his arms and devour her lips for a very long time.

"Why do you look so deep in thought?" she asked, breaking into his salacious thoughts.

"You look very pretty."

"I do? I'm not wearing any makeup."

"You don't need any, and I'm serious."

"Gee, thanks. That's such a lovely thing to say."

A soft pink blush crossed her face.

He felt almost hypnotized.

Reluctantly shifting his gaze, he turned his attention back to his cooking, and a few minutes later, he plated the french toast.

"Let's sit in a booth," he suggested, setting two large dishes and the stack on a tray. "Would you grab the coffee pot?"

"Sure, but Connor, that looks and smells amazing."

"I hope it is," he said as he walked into the tavern.

Choosing a booth next to a window so he could keep watch, he placed the French Toast in the middle of the table. Picking up a slice and smothering it with maple syrup, she took a bite and rolled her eyes.

"This is incredible," she exclaimed. "Where did you learn to cook like this?"

"Mabel," he replied. "She was the cook when I bought this place, and she still is. I could barely boil an egg when I started out. Now I'm pretty handy around a kitchen."

"I must thank Mabel," Colleen said with a grin. "You'll make some woman very happy one of these days."

"I hope so, but April, can you tell me why were you so scared last night?"

He watched her carefully.

She dropped her eyes, took another mouthful of her breakfast, then laid her fork on the plate.

"Connor, I don't want you caught up in my problems."

"Whatever they are, I'm happy to get caught up in them," he replied solemnly. "I want to help."

"But, why? You don't even know me. I'm a complete stranger."

He took a breath.

How could he tell her she'd been haunting his every waking hour since she'd left his bar a month before?

"Did you do something criminal, besides borrow a car, I mean?"

"No, absolutely not, and I only borrowed it because I had to," she said earnestly, then glanced across at the bar.

"I want to tell you something," she began, turning back to face him. "You probably don't remember me, but about a month ago I stopped in here and had a beer."

"Of course I remember you!"

"You do?" she exclaimed happily, the heavy crease across her brow fading away. "It was super busy, but you were so friendly."

"It wasn't hard," he quipped with a grin. "Is that what you wanted to tell me?"

"Yes and no, the thing is, when I jumped in that car and took off last night, I was on my way to this place. Even though it was really late, I had this weird feeling you'd be here and you'd let me in. I'd planned to park the car out of sight somewhere, so it wouldn't be seen in your parking lot. The thing is, a month ago, when I was sitting at the bar, I, uh, I really liked you, and you've been on my mind ever since."

"I thought you were pretty special yourself, April," he said, barely able to contain his excitement, "and I've been thinking about you too. I tried to find out who you were, but no-one had any idea."

"Really?"

"Hell, yeah. Why do you sound so surprised?"

"I, uh, I didn't think you'd be single. You are, right? It seems like you are."

"Yeah, I'm single. Very single."

"I think I just got my Christmas present," she said softly, tilting her head to the side and grinning at him.

"Me too," he replied, wanting to take her up to his bedroom and unwrap her. "I'm going to a Christmas dinner this afternoon. Will you join me?"

"I'd love it, but are you sure I won't be intruding?"

"One-hundred percent sure, and between now and then, you can tell me what's goin' on."

"But Connor, I meant what I said. I don't want you getting tangled up in my mess."

"Let me hear about it, and we'll take things from there, okay?"

"Okay, and thank you, thank you for everything."

"I think I know someone who could use a hug."

"Yes, please."

Walking around to her side of the booth, he helped her to her feet and wrapped her up. As her body melted against his, he closed his eyes and said a silent prayer of thanks.

CHAPTER THREE

Sinking into Connor's protective, muscled arms, April believed as long as she was with him she'd be safe. When she'd escaped from the Churchill Chateau, which she now thought of as the House of Horrors, the snowstorm had been raging. Though she had no friends in the small town, a month before she'd stopped at a tavern called McBrides Bar. The bartender, a gorgeous cowboy she'd guessed to be the owner, had been warm and inviting. In spite of the busy night, he'd taken time to chat, and the attraction had been immediate. Fleeing the chateau and driving frantically through the frightening night, she'd headed to the tavern. Though it was a long shot, a voice inside her head had pushed her forward, insisting she'd find a safe haven with the cowboy who had been on her mind since they'd met.

"Feelin' better?" Connor murmured, slowly pulling back.

"So much better. Thank you. I think my insides have finally stopped shaking."

"Let's clear up these breakfast things, then go up to my livin' room and you can tell me all about it."

"I'd like that," she replied, looking up at him. "I'd like that very much."

As they puttered around the kitchen her mood began to lighten. Connor had a keen wit, their banter was fun and comfortable, but as they made their way up the winding staircase, and she thought about her narrow escape, a chill pricked her skin.

"I'm not sure where to begin," she said thoughtfully as they settled on the couch.

"What brought you to this town? It's not exactly on the beaten path?"

"I came to look at a horse at the Churchill stables. It's a long drive from where I live, about five hours, but when I looked at the pictures of the Yellow Inn, I thought it would be fun. I've never stayed at a bed and breakfast, and the timing was right. I needed a break."

"When was that?"

"About a month ago, when I came in for that drink and we met. I'd had dinner at the Chateau, and I saw this place driving back to the inn. The only reason I didn't stay was because I had to get up early for the drive home. To be honest, I almost left you my phone number, but it seemed—sort of—pushy, and I'm not like that. I wish I had, but I knew I'd be coming back. The Churchills have some really nice horses."

"I guess things didn't pan out the way you thought they would."

"Good grief, they sure as hell didn't," she said with a heavy sigh. "About a week after I got home, one of the sons contacted me about coming back. Did you know there are five brothers in the Churchill family, and they're all named after English Kings?"

"I knew the five brothers part, but not that they're named after kings. That's bizarre."

"You have no idea," she muttered, rolling her eyes. "Henry is the father, and while I was at that awful house, I wondered if he just calls himself Henry in honor of Henry the Eighth. He's so creepy and dictatorial. Anyway, there's Charles, William, James, Richard, and the youngest is Edward. It was Richard who called me. He was extremely nice on the phone. We started to Skype and email, and it became personal. I'm going to say something now because I have to," she said looking at Connor intently. "The whole time this was going on, I was thinking about coming back here so I could see you again."

"And I was prayin' you'd walk through that door."

"You have no idea how happy that makes me," she replied, leaning against his shoulder. "Anyway, the Chateau is huge. It's over twenty-thousand square feet, and—"

"Did you say twenty-thousand square feet?" he exclaimed, interrupting her.

"I know, incredible, isn't it?"

"Don't they get lost?"

"There are a lot of Churchill's in that place."

"I'm sorry, I interrupted you," Connor apologized. "Please, keep goin.'"

"I did have some clients interested in a couple of horses I'd seen there, so I agreed to come back to ride and video them. Richard invited me to stay. It made sense, but it was my first big mistake."

"The first?"

"They offered to fly me down in their jet, and I said yes to that as well."

"Ah, I see. That put you at their mercy. You didn't have your car."

"Right," she muttered, her voice full of regret. "The first couple of days were okay, a bit weird, but okay, and that's when I made the third, and biggest, mistake. I agreed to stay through Christmas Eve. What happened next was—good grief— it's so difficult to explain everything."

"Why?"

"It will sound like I'm describing a bad dream, and believe me, it was, except the nightmare was real."

"Don't worry about how it sounds just tell me."

"There's just so much. The three older sons are married and have young children. They all live in the house. The wives, they were nice at first, but then they started peppering me with questions about my life. Nosey questions, inappropriate questions, and the kids weren't like normal kids. They didn't run around and play. They were always very serious, as if they were afraid to say or do anything wrong. Then every time I turned around, Edward was staring at me. I have no idea why. When I mentioned it to Richard he told me I should be flattered."

"You can't be serious."

"I'm totally serious. Things started getting worse. If I said I was going down to the stables, Richard would drop whatever he was doing and come with me, and while I was there, he didn't let me out of their sight. If I asked to be driven into town, there'd be some reason not to take me. Whenever I left my room, one of the brothers appeared in the hallway and started walking with me. When I told Richard I wanted to leave, he said the jet wouldn't be available for a few days, I decided to rent a car. He got really agitated and said his parents would get very upset because I'd committed to stay through Christmas Eve and I couldn't just bail."

"You felt you had to stay?"

"No! Not at all, I didn't care about his creepy parents, but I told him I'd stay just to calm him down and call my father. He's a lawyer, and he can get heavy, if you know what I mean. I knew he'd send a car for me, or do something. At this point I was freaking out."

"What did your dad say?"

"I couldn't find my cell phone," she said, taking a sharp breath. "I'd left it on my dresser, but I found it in my purse."

"I'm not even going to ask if you might have made a mistake," Connor said gravely. "Did you call your dad then?"

"I was scared they'd put some kind of listening device in it, and I know that sounds totally crazy, but—"

"I don't think it sounds crazy at all!"

"A part of me thought I was being ridiculous. Why would they hurt me? Mom and dad knew I was there, all my friends knew I was there, so I decided I'd stick around until Christmas Eve, then get the hell out of there."

"But something happened."

April slowly nodded, then suddenly dropped her head in her hands.

"My God, what is it?" Connor asked putting his arm around her shoulders. "What did these lunatics do?"

"I'm sorry. It's just—talking about what happened—it's not easy."

"Take your time."

"I'm okay," she said taking a deep breath. "Everyone was at dinner, and each of the children had three presents in front of them. They opened a gift after each course. They said thank you, and that was it. So weird."

"Was there a cook? Were the meals served?"

"The three wives did everything."

"I see, go on."

"After dinner we all went into the living room for coffee, and the wives took the kids away, and it was me, Anne, Henry, and the brothers. They had this punch. Apparently it was a tradition, and Anne insisted I join in. I took a sip, and I swear, Connor, it had this really weird taste. I was sitting next to a potted plant, thank God, and every chance I could I'd tip some out, but I pretended that I was getting wasted. When the cup was finally empty, I excused myself to visit the bathroom and acted like I was staggering out of the room. I opened and closed the powder room door loudly, so they'd hear it, then crept back and stood outside the door so I could listen."

"You're a smart, brave girl, April."

"Thank you, but not really. I knew they were planning something, and I had to find out what it was."

"I'm almost afraid to hear what came next," Connor mumbled. "I can't believe you went through this."

"Buckle up," she said dramatically. "Henry told everyone to stand up and raise their glasses to toast Richard's new wife. Everyone repeated it, then Anne said she was leaving to prepare the bridal suite."

"Oh, my, God."

"I bolted to my room, grabbed my heavy coat and my purse and ran to the garage. They have so many cars. They're all numbered and the keys are kept in a cabinet by the door. I threw them into the meat freezer, except one set of course, and jumped in that car."

"Damn, girl, that was brilliant."

"I don't know about that, but it was the only thing I could think of to stop them following me, or at least give me a head start. The seconds it took for that garage door to roll up were the longest seconds of my life. I pulled out just as they came running into the garage. I knew the car had a remote for the front gate so I wasn't worried about that. Connor, from the moment I got behind the steering wheel, I was headed for this place. It was so late, but I knew you'd be here, and I'd be safe. It was so strange."

"You know what's even stranger?" he murmured, putting his arm around her shoulders. "I stayed in town for Christmas because I knew you were comin' back. Don't ask me how I knew, but I did, and I had to stay put. But what happened to the car?"

"I lost control around a bend and ended up in a ditch. I couldn't stick around in case they were after me, so I started walking. I lost my purse somewhere along the way, but I don't know how I made it. It took forever. When I reached your door and it was open, I was so happy, but I was on my last legs. The minute I stepped inside I collapsed."

"I don't know what to say, but I'm sure glad we both listened to whatever it was that was guidin' us."

"Me too," she said with a sigh, leaning against him. "I think I was about to be brainwashed to be a perfect mate for Richard. It's right out of The Stepford Wives."

"I can't imagine anyone brainwashin' you," he said skeptically.

"Who knows, but what happens now? I don't think they did anything criminal, and even if they did, it would be my word against theirs. I'm still a bit scared. They won't want me blabbing about their life."

"You need a couple of days to catch your breath. Do you want me to take you straight to the airport and put you on a plane?"

"I doubt I'd be able to get a flight. It's Christmas, and there are storms everywhere."

"Good point, but you need to call your family and let them know you're okay and you'll be home soon."

"Definitely, though I won't tell them what happened. I don't want to ruin their Christmas."

"That's up to you, but you're safe now. I won't let anything happen to you."

"Connor," she murmured, grabbing his arm, "you saved me."

* * *

Connor's heart swelled, but hearing the story, he was worried the Churchill brothers would return. They needed to leave.

"I'm going to clear the driveway," he declared. "Why don't you call your folks, then we'll go to my home. If those Churchill's do come back, they'll find McBride's Bar and Grill closed up and empty."

But she didn't move.

Chemistry between them crackled.

She was waiting for the inevitable kiss.

Leaning forward, he watched her eyes flutter closed.

As he pressed his mouth against hers, she moved her arms around his neck, fervently responding to his kiss. His fingers sliding into her hair, he devoured her mouth with hungry passion, and when he finally pulled back, she fell breathlessly against him. Holding her tightly, he couldn't find his voice.

"April," he finally muttered, "I think, if I don't shovel that snow right now...."

"I know," she whispered. "You'd better go. They could come back."

He kissed her again, lightly and quickly, then rose to his feet.

"The phone's over there," he said pointing to a small desk in the corner of the room. "I'll be back in a bit."

* * *

Watching him stride away, admiring his wide shoulders and the bulging biceps wanting to burst through his tight black sweater, she flashed back to the night before.

When she'd stood in the doorway of his living room after her shower, he'd been laying on the couch naked from the waist up. Though she'd been bone weary, the sight of his ripped abdomen and strong arms had sent a warm thrill through her body. Now she'd felt his touch and experienced his kiss, she was totally hooked. But she knew the Churchill's would hunt her down...

CHAPTER FOUR

Connor had cleared the driveway, April's coat had dried overnight, and she was safely ensconced in his 4WD SUV, but as he was about to pull out of the garage, he had a sudden thought.

"I think you should duck down. Those damn Churchill's might be cruisin' around lookin' for you."

"Do you think I should call Richard and let him know I'm okay and where the car is?"

"That's not a bad idea, but I think you should text him, not call. Do you have your phone?"

"I know I grabbed it when I left the house, but I can't remember if it was in my bag or if I left it in the car. I wouldn't trust it now anyway."

"You can use mine. I'll just turn off my caller ID."

Pulling his phone from his pocket and blocking his information, he handed it across to her.

"What should I write?" she asked, scrunching down as Connor rolled down the driveway.

"Tell him it's you, and you don't want to hear from him, then give him the location of the car."

"Okay, how's this?" she asked as she typed out the message.

Richard, it's April. Don't try to reach me. Your car is on the Ellison Highway near the Five Peaks turnoff.

"Perfect," Connor replied.

She hit SEND, and moments later received a reply.

April, I'm so sorry if I upset you somehow, but you shouldn't have run off. Tell me where you are. I'll pick you up and we can talk.

"Asshole," she muttered.

"What did he say?"

"That I should tell him where I am so he can pick me up and we can talk. I'll talk to him all right," she said angrily, then typed a response and read it out loud.

How stupid do you think I am? I borrowed a car and bolted because I overheard your father toasting me as your new wife, and your mother saying she was leaving to prepare the bridal suite. Don't ever contact me again.

"I'm not sure you should tell him you overheard that conversation."

"I want to," she exclaimed, and before Connor could respond she hit the SEND button.

"Thank you," she said with a relieved, satisfied sigh as she handed the phone back to him. "That felt good."

"I guess all the cards are on the table now," he remarked, dropping the phone in his jacket pocket, "but you didn't tell me you walked all the way from the Five Peak turnoff. How the heck did you manage that?"

"Slowly," she mumbled, shivering at the memory.

"You must have had an angel on your shoulder to make it all the way to the tavern."

"Maybe I did," she said softly. "Maybe it's a Christmas miracle."

It was only five minutes to the town's main street, and driving past the shops, he saw a few people strolling along wearing Santa hats and enjoying the rare sunny day.

Every Christmas, the town's diner opened its doors for a few short hours. As Connor approached, he was startled to see a white Range Rover with the license plate 5CCHILL parked out front.

"April, I've just spotted the white Range Rover."

"You're kidding?"

"Nope," he muttered, moving slowly past and staring at the restaurant's windows. "The brothers, do they have short black hair?" he asked, spotting the two men at a booth staring intently out into the street.

"Yes, all the brothers had exactly the same haircut."

"They're in Bert's Diner."

"There's a diner open on Christmas day?"

"Bert opens it every year from ten until around one."

"Are you sure it's them?" she asked, panic in her voice. "Sorry, stupid question. You've never seen them. How could you know?"

"It's their Range Rover parked out front. I'm gonna pull over."

"What? Why?"

"There may be another way to handle this," he said thoughtfully, driving a short distance down the block before pulling into the curb. "Maybe they'll leave you alone if they see you've got a friend in town."

"But, Connor, doesn't that family have a lot of influence around here?"

"Yes and no. They spend most of their money in Clearview. That's half-an-hour in the opposite direction. There's a mall there with big name department stores."

"I know all about that mall," she remarked with a frown. "Richard took me there. The next day just about everything I'd said I liked arrived on the doorstep."

"Damn."

"It was ridiculous."

"If you don't wanna go in, it's okay, but hear me out. These guys are bullies, and the best way to beat a bully is to push back. The other thing, and this is even more important, if they see us together they'll know you're not here by yourself. Like I said earlier, it might make them back off. As far as them havin' influence, I've got a lotta friends in this place too, good friends, important friends. Are you game? You wanna get some coffee and pie?"

"Screw them!" she exclaimed defiantly. "Yes, I'm game! I'd love some coffee and pie, well, coffee anyway. I'm not sure I could handle any pie after that delicious breakfast."

"I hear that," he said with a chuckle. "Let's walk. No reason they should know what kinda car I drive."

"Are you worried?"

"Not at all, I'm just bein' smart about things."

"You're right again," she quipped. "It's becoming a habit."

"Yep, one you should get used to."

She shot him a look, then grinned, climbing from the car.

"So much for not wanting to be seen," she muttered, as he took her hand and they started up the street.

"Are you having second thoughts?"

"Not really, but I am nervous."

"You're with a cowboy, darlin'. Cowboy's know how to take care of smarmy boys like them."

"I don't doubt it for a second."

He squeezed her hand.

"One thing," he continued, "and it's important. If they come up, look out the window. Totally ignore them. Let me do the talkin', okay?"

"Okay."

"Nothing escalates things more than the girl speakin' up."

"How do you know?"

"Watchin' from behind my bar, I've seen plenty."

"Oh, right, I bet you have."

"So remember, if they approach, sit there quiet as a church mouse and stare out that window. No eye contact, nothin'."

"Okay, cowboy, I won't look, and I won't make a peep."

Reaching the door to the restaurant, April stood back as Connor pushed it open and walked inside first.

"Hi, Connor," the waitress said with a warm smile. "Merry Christmas."

"Merry Christmas to you too, Becky. Can I have that booth by the window at the end?" he asked, wanting to walk past the Churchill brothers.

"Sure, come on back."

Making sure he was between April and tables, he gripped her hand and followed the waitress. As they neared the two men one of them casually glanced up, and Connor caught his startled look.

"April!"

She ignored him, and they continued on, but Connor felt her fingers tighten in his hand. Reaching the booth and removing their coats, he made sure she sat with her back to them, then settled opposite her. As Becky placed the menus on the table and moved away, Connor saw one of the brothers stand up and stride towards them.

"April, we're about to have a visitor," Connor muttered. "Remember what I said. Look out the window. Completely ignore him no matter what he says."

Connor studied the menu pretending not to notice the man's approach.

"Hello, April."

Lifting his gaze, Connor studied his opponent.

The man was average in build and height, but his anger was obvious. Connor didn't doubt he could take him, but if he could intimidate the man verbally everyone would be better off.

"The young lady doesn't wish to speak to you," Connor said calmly.

"I'm Richard Churchill! Maybe you've heard of me and my family?"

"Nope, can't say I have," Connor replied, holding his gaze. "Not that it would matter, now please leave."

"I don't know who you are," Richard snarled, leaning forward, "and I don't give a shit, but April is coming home with me."

"Here's the thing, Dick," Connor said firmly, his stare unwavering. "If you don't walk away, I'm gonna have to hurt you, and I'd rather not do that. Don't get me wrong, it would give me a great deal of pleasure to pound my fist into your nose, but there are some real nice people here enjoyin' a happy Christmas mornin', some with their kids, and I'd rather not spoil that. So—Dick—you need to walk away—now."

"The name is Richard, and like I said, April is coming home with me."

"I'm gonna count to three," Connor said, narrowing his eyes. "If you're still standin' there..."

"Meet me around the back," Richard hissed, and with a last glare at April, he marched away.

"Dick, you called him, Dick," she said in a hushed whisper, shifting her eyes from the window. "I couldn't believe my ears."

"His name is Dick, and he is a dick. If the shoe fits..."

"I'm shaking like a leaf right now."

"I reckon I can fix that."

Swiftly scooting around the booth and sitting next to her, he pulled her into his arms and kissed her. Not a light, quick peck, but a deep, loving, gliding of the lips that took her breath away.

"Oh, my gosh," she panted as they broke apart, "you're amazing."

"Darlin', amazin' is walkin' through a snow storm to get to my door."

"Please don't go around the back and fight them."

"I'm not goin' anywhere. If he wants to assume I'm goin' back there, that's up to him."

"Do you think they're waiting for you?"

"Like a couple of morons, and they're gonna have a long wait," he replied with a grin.

"But won't that tick them off even more?"

"April," he said patiently, "they're ticked off at you, sure, but now they're gonna be even more ticked off at me. They don't know it, but their focus is already shiftin', and that's what I wanted."

"I don't want the Churchill family ticked off at you!"

"Shush. I knew plenty of guys like him back in the city. They're all the same. At some point they'll get bored and go away."

"Have you decided?"

Looking up, Connor smiled at the young waitress.

"Sorry, Becky, I didn't see you there. Coffee, and one slice of your apple-rhubarb pie. Make it hot, with a scoop of ice-cream."

"You got it."

"Can I have tea?" April piped up.

"Sure," Becky said with a grin. "I like that pie with tea myself. I'll be right back."

"Tea?" Connor repeated, raising his eyebrows.

"Coffee peps me up. Tea calms me down."

"I'll remember that, and now," he murmured, landing a quick kiss, "I'm movin' back on the other side so I can look at you."

"But I like sitting close to you like this."

"I don't wanna spoil you, cos if I spoil you," he murmured, pausing dramatically, "I'll have to spank you."

Tilting her head to the side, she looked at him intently.

"What if I threw a tantrum?"

Connor took a breath.

Was it possible?

Could anything be so absolutely, totally perfect?

"If you threw a tantrum," he whispered, his lips at her ear, "I'd have to spank you hard, real hard."

He heard her gasp.

With his cock stirring, he quickly moved to sit across from her.

* * *

April could already imagine being draped over his lap as his hard hand swatted her backside. She'd experienced the stunning, sparkling pleasure of an erotic spanking only once, and she'd loved it. As her heart raced like a thoroughbred galloping on the track, and a hot flush crept across her face, she stared across the table at him.

His eyes blazed back at her.

He'd meant every word.

CHAPTER FIVE

Connor had watched the brothers leave the diner, but even though he and April had taken their time enjoying the pie, the Range Rover was still parked out front.

"They're waiting," April remarked with a worried frown. "Maybe we should call the sheriff."

"And say what? Nothing's happened."

"Do you think it was a mistake coming in here?"

"Not at all, they know you have protection now."

"Then why are they still here?"

"They're arrogant. They probably think they can intimidate me by followin' us when we leave. We're gonna cross the street and stay away from my car."

"Why?"

"Cos if something happens and I have to hurt them, I don't want you watchin'."

"I don't understand."

"You will."

"I'm so glad I'm with you."

"Back at ya," he replied with a wink. "Just do what I say when I say it, okay?"

"Okay, cowboy," she quipped, winking back at him.

"Let's go."

Pulling on their coats, they headed outside, turned right, rather than left towards his car, and crossed the road.

"Why do you want to be on this side of the street?"

"There are more storefronts with windows," he replied, pausing in front of a boutique. "I'm able to see what's behind us."

"You're brilliant!"

"Not really. I just know about this stuff, and look, there they are."

"Now I'm suddenly scared," she muttered, seeing the brothers re-flected as they walked across the street towards them.

"Hey, darlin', they're the one's who should be scared," he muttered, placing his arm around her shoulders and guiding her up the block. "We're goin' to that break between the stores."

"April, wait up!" one of the brothers yelled. "Hang on a second. I just want to talk to you."

"Keep walkin'," Connor said firmly. "Whatever you do, don't turn around, and when my arm leaves your shoulder, walk, don't run, walk, into that small opening between the stores and wait, but no matter what you hear, don't peek around. Got it?"

"Connor..."

"When I drop my arm, go straight there, and no lookin' back, not even for a second. I'll be with you before you know it."

"Okay. Shit, shit, shit."

* * *

A moment later, Connor's arm fell from her shoulder.

Her heart thumping and fighting the overwhelming temptation to turn around, she walked briskly forward and slipped into the narrow pathway.

But as the seconds ticked by, her desperate need got the better of her. With her back flat against the wall, she poked her head around. Both brothers were on the ground, one doubled over, the other with his hands covering his face, and Connor was striding towards her.

"I told you not to look," he scolded, grabbing her elbow and bustling her down the path.

"I'm sorry, I couldn't help it."

"Obviously."

Reaching the end of the narrow lane, he turned down the alley be-hind the shops.

"Why didn't you want me—?"

"We'll talk about it later," he said sternly, cutting her off.

It was a short walk to the next break between buildings, and as they approached he slowed his step.

"April, stay behind me as we walk back up to the street. Their Rover should be gone by now, but until I know for sure, you need to stay outta sight."

"How do you know they'll take off?"

"They're babies. They'll be runnin' home to their momma, or the urgent care at the other end of town. Either way, they don't have the stomach to stick around and deal with me again."

"You're amazing," she said breathlessly. "I know I've said that before, but it's true."

Smiling down at her, he pressed his lips to her ear.

"I'm not sure how amazin' you'll think I am when you're over my knee gettin' your ass spanked."

She stared up at him, utterly speechless, as a bevy of butterflies burst to life in her stomach.

"This time, do as I say," he continued. "Stay behind me. I need to make sure the coast is clear."

Her face flaming red, she managed to nod, then followed him up the lane.

"Stay here," he muttered as he neared the sidewalk. "I need to get against that opposite wall so I can see the front of the diner. It's gonna make me visible to that side of the street. If they're still around or gettin' in their car, they might spot me, which doesn't bother me, but I don't want them seein' you. Got it?"

"Uh-huh."

"You're gonna stay put?"

"Yes, I promise," she said earnestly, his threat of a spanking hovering over her head.

Her heart racing, she watched him step across the lane, narrow his eyes, and peer across the street. Finally walking out to the sidewalk, he looked in both directions, then to her great relief he signaled her to join him.

"Looks like they're gone," he declared as she reached his side.

"Why aren't we going to the car?"

"Just smellin' the wind."

"What do you mean, smelling the wind? There is no wind."

"Shush."

Standing quietly studying him, she began to think Connor McBride was a whole lot more than just a cowboy who owned a bar.

"I spent some time up in Alaska with an Indian tracker," he murmured, taking her hand. "The guy was unbelievable. He taught me how to smell the wind. It means usin' my senses to pick up the energy of my prey, in this case, my enemy. They've left. He also taught me how to think fight."

"Which means...?"

"Reading your opponent, anticipating his next move and being ready for it when it comes. You can't do that if you're emotional. Come on, let's go home."

Walking with her across the street, his fingers curled firmly around hers, they reached his SUV and headed off to his house. Though she kept looking behind them, there was no sign of the white Range Rover. As he continued out of town, she noticed the homes were spread apart, most set on large parcels. Turning up a gentle slope, she glanced out the window and let out a low whistle.

"This view is fantastic, and look at all the horses," she declared. "How many do you have?"

"Two, Mitch and Molly, brother and sister. They were here when I bought this place and I was happy to let them stay."

"How do you take care of them? Aren't you at the tavern all the time?"

"There's a teenager next door who loves them to bits. Her name's Suzy, and she's been their best friend for years. I pay her to keep doin' what she was doin' for free. I feed them in the mornin' and open the barn door, but she gives them their supplements, blankets, mucks their stalls and paddock. They go in and out as they please. I just close it at night to keep other critters out."

"How old are they?"

"Apparently twenty-two, but I can't swear by it. They're more human than horse. But I'm itchin' to make this place into a working ranch. There's a rundown facility behind me, almost ten acres. The owner told me he'll be lookin' to move it soon. I'm gonna buy it, at least, that's the plan. I just don't know how I'll do it. The transition will be tough."

"Transition?

"I can't run the tavern and rebuild a ranch. They're both full-time jobs. Do I lease the tavern? Do I sell it? It's a big question mark."

"You'll figure it out."

"Yep, and I take it you ride. Didn't you say you were at the Churchill estate lookin' at horses?"

"Yes, I help people find what they're looking for, and I couldn't live without my mare," she replied, thinking about her mare. "I miss her like crazy."

"I wanna hear all about her," he said, turning into a driveway. "Heck, April, I wanna hear all about you."

"Connor, your home is incredible," she exclaimed as he stopped in front of wrought iron gates.

"I wouldn't say it's incredible, but I'm happy comin' here every night."

The gates swung open, and he drove slowly forward into a double garage. The house was a traditional two-story with eaves, and sat behind a six foot high, natural rock fence.

"The wall, it looks old."

"It is—very," he replied. "It was crumblin' when I bought this place, but I liked it so much I had it repaired. It's solid now, and it gives the house privacy. I'm gonna call my ranch Grey Stone Farms in honor of that wall," he said proudly, rolling into the garage, "and I plan to build a natural stone facade around the barn."

"That sounds fantastic."

"Are you sure you wanna go inside the Connor Castle? You never know, it might be like the Churchill Chateau."

"Don't even joke about that," she retorted, rolling her eyes. "Although..."

"Go on."

"Never mind," she said, suppressing a giggle as she thought about enjoying a bridal suite in his home.

Climbing from the SUV and following him into the house, she found herself in a hallway with polished wood floors, and vintage horse prints lining the walls.

"I'll give you the tour. You have your choice of the downstairs guest room, or the one upstairs."

"Thank you so much for letting me stay with you," she said gratefully as they moved through the foyer into the living room.

"Are you kiddin'? I'm happy you're here."

But she'd stopped short to stare at the natural rock fireplace.

"Wow, Connor, it's beautiful, and it matches the wall."

"Yep, I had to renovate the insides of it, but all that masonry is original."

"You should name this place Grey Stone Manor."

"Hey, that's not a bad idea."

As he took her from room to room, then up the stairs, she was impressed by his flair for decorating. Stunning antiques were artfully interspersed with traditional, comfortable furniture, but when he opened the door to his master bedroom, she caught her breath. A heavily carved, four-post, Tudor bed boasting old-world splendor, sat in the center.

"Where did you find this?" she asked, running her fingers across the intricate carvings.

"An antique mall goin' outta business. The frame had some damage and the dealer needed a quick sale. I wanted it the minute I set eyes on it."

"I don't blame you."

"April..." but as she turned and looked at him, his voice trailed off.

* * *

Her eyes held a longing, a hunger, a need to be taken, and he ached to give her what she craved. He wanted to travel his hands across her body, suck her nipples and nuzzle her neck.

"A penny for your thoughts?" he murmured, ambling slowly towards her.

"I think what's going through my head is worth a bit more than that."

"Such a sassy girl," he said with a sigh, digging his hand into his pocket.

"A nickel," he declared, holding it up. "Five pennies, five thoughts, what's the first?"

"I think you want to kiss me, and I'd like that very much."

Wordlessly placing both hands on either side of her face, he languidly glided his mouth over hers, then sucked in her lower lip.

"Second thought?" he asked softly as he pulled back.

"You just numbed my brain."

"That was a lie. Second thought."

"I think your house is fabulous."

"Thanks. Third?"

"I think you want me naked."

Her voice had fallen into a whisper.

"Do you want to be naked?"

"Uh-huh, but, um..."

"But what?"

"Isn't it too soon?"

"Do you want to be naked?" he repeated. "The truth."

"Uh-huh."

"Do you want to be naked now?"

"Yes, please."

Lifting her sweater, he tickled her waist.

Her eyelids fluttered, and he heard a quiet moan.

"Next thought?" he insisted, pressing his palm against the small of her back.

"Why didn't you want me to look when I was between those shops?"

"You were a very naughty girl."

"I know," she breathed, dropping her head on to his shoulder, "but will you tell me?"

* * *

Her heart thudded against her chest.

Wetness flooded her sex.

His fingers sparked her skin.

She ached for him to pull off her sweater, throw her on the bed and ravage her.

"Because," he softly began, "they may press charges against me. You can't testify to something you didn't see happen, or the aftermath of what happened."

"Oh, no, I'm sorry. Can I ask why you wanted me to walk and not run?"

"If you run, you could trip and fall over. At least you did that part right."

"I'm an idiot. I shouldn't have looked around."

"You're forgiven, now tell me your fifth and last thought."

She paused.

"I'm waitin."

"Are you, uh, really, uh..."

"Am I really, what?"

"I can't say it."

"Am I really gonna spank you for not listenin'?"

She nodded her head.

"I sure am, darlin', but you're gonna have to crawl over my lap and ask for it."

CHAPTER SIX

Staring into April's wide, surprised eyes, Connor took her hand, led her around the bed, and sat on the edge of the mattress. Staring down at him expectantly, she began fidgeting, then dropped her gaze to the floor.

"Don't you have a question for me?" he finally asked. "I'm not gonna sit here all day."

"Uh, please will you, uh, spank me?" she muttered. "Shit, I can't believe I just said that."

"There's still time to change your mind. Three-seconds to be exact. One-two-three. No? Okay," he said firmly, tugging her forward. "Over my lap."

"Oh, my gosh," she stammered, falling over his knees. "Shit shit, shit."

"Stop it!" he declared, landing a sudden slap. "What makes you believe I'm not a man of my word?"

"Nothing...shit...I can't think."

"You just gave me five thoughts for a nickel."

"No, you don't understand."

"Then tell me," he said, fondling her backside.

"Your hand, while you're doing what you're doing, I can't think."

"I see. Well, April, that's how it should be. The thinkin' starts afterwards, when your butt is burnin' and you're feelin' sorry. Are you ready?"

"I guess."

"Nope, that's not good enough," he retorted. "Why are you over my knee about to have your butt smacked?"

"Because I didn't listen," she whimpered. "I'm sorry about that, honest."

"And?"

"There's an and?"

"Because it's something you want, right?"

"Ooh, Connor."

"Answer me," he insisted, landing another slap..

"Yes, yes, because it's something I want."

"There you go. Let's try that again. Are you ready?"

"Yes, I'm ready."

Though she'd squeaked her reply, Connor had no doubt her heart was pounding with excitement, and if he touched between her legs he'd find her gloriously wet. Raising his hand, he delivered three solid smacks on each cheek.

Her only response was a slight wiggle.

He repeated them.

As she let out a restrained, *ouch,* he increased the speed of his slaps, moving his hand from cheek to cheek with gusto until she yowled loudly and threw her hand behind her.

"Ow, ow, Connor, that stings!"

"Of course it does. Stand up and take off your jeans."

"Seriously?"

He responded with a rapid volley of sharp swats.

"Does that answer your question?"

"Yes, yes, okay, okay," she exclaimed urgently, pushing herself off his lap.

"I'm spankin' you for not listenin', and what do you do? Question my instruction," he declared, shaking his head.

"Sorry," she mumbled breathlessly, unzipping her jeans and pulling them off.

"Mmm, nice panties," he murmured, staring at the black lace underwear.

"Uh, thank you, I'm glad you like them," she said awkwardly, staring at the floor.

"Back on over my knee."

"More? But my butt is already stinging."

"April...," he said shaking his head, "are you just after a real hard spankin'. Is that it? You want me to set your ass on fire?"

"No, I'm just, uh..."

"Used to doin' what you want? Are you a spoiled brat underneath all that sweet sugar?"

"Sometimes," she whispered dropping her eyes, "maybe just a bit."

"You know that's not gonna fly with me, right?"

"Apparently."

"Oh, Lord, I can see you're gonna be walkin' around with a sore backside more often than not," he exclaimed, grabbing her wrist and yanking her back over his lap.

"Connor, I—!"

"You'd better not say anything you'll regret," he warned, sliding her panties down and dispatching his palm across her naked glowing cheeks, "not while you're in this position."

* * *

April was shocked.

He'd exposed her so fast she hadn't had time to react, and suddenly he was smacking her naked bottom with hard, hot slaps. She squirmed and wailed in protest, but his hold around her waist was too strong. With one arm pinned against his body, she tried throwing the other hand behind her, but he grabbed her wrist and held it at the small of her back.

"I'm sorry, I'm sorry," she howled. "I'll be good, I swear, I'll listen, I will, please, please, no more."

To her great relief the smacks stopped.

"Oh, my, God," she bleated. "You spanked me so hard."

"Not really," he said calmly, smoothing his hand over her scorched skin. "Just enough to make my point and get your attention."

"Ooh, but it's burning and all prickly."

"Uh-huh, and you can count on it bein' that way again if you don't mind me. Have you got anything to say?"

"Like what?"

"Like, thanking me for takin' you in hand like you wanted."

"I'm not sure I wanted quite so much."

"Whoa! Is that a complaint?"

"No, no, sorry."

"When I spank you, darlin', I'm gonna spank you like I think you need it, and from the sounds of it, you need more."

"No! No! I don't! Honest!"

"You've got a real sassy mouth on you, and it's cute, I like it, but if you push the envelope too much, your ass will be redder and stingin' a whole lot more than it is right now. Understand?"

"I understand," she whimpered with a heavy, resigned sigh.

"Now tell me honestly, are you happy about that?"

"Uh-huh."

"Are you sure? That didn't sound convincin'."

"I am, honestly. It's just hard to admit."

"Now you have, so we know where we stand," he said, softening his voice.

Helping her on to the bed, he stretched out beside her and took her in his arms.

"My gosh, Connor, I don't know what to say."

"I thought you told me you'd been spanked before. Did I hear you wrong?"

"No, but it was just once, and it wasn't like that."

"What was it like?"

"We were having sex and I was on my hand and knees. It was amazing. Ever since I've wondered what it would be like to, uh..."

"Be spanked properly?"

"Yeah..."

He'd been continuing to rub away the sting, but nuzzling her neck, he slipped his fingers between her legs. She was saturated. Hastily pulling her sweater over her head, he gazed down at the black lace bra covering her breasts. Deciding to leave it in place for the moment, he climbed off the bed and hastily undressed.

* * *

Slightly dazed, her bottom deliciously hot and stinging, April gazed at Connor as he peeled off his clothes. His six pack and heavily muscled arms suggested hours in a gym, but she suspected it was from years of lifting heavy boxes in his bar and renovating his home. She couldn't wait to be engulfed by him, to have his rigid cock slide inside her hungry pussy, and feel his powerful body crushing hers. He smiled down at her, a crooked, wicked smile, and as he climbed back on the bed, she opened her arms.

"Hey, darlin'," he murmured, accepting her hug. "Do you need some lovin'?"

"More than I ever have in my life."

His lips found her neck, and as he kissed his way to her shoulders, she moaned in pleasure, but as he moved his hand inside her bra and kneaded her breast, she let out a cry.

"Damn, girl, I wanna search out every inch of you and tongue you for hours."

His wicked words sent a fresh sizzle through her sex, and she groaned loudly as he traveled his mouth down to her chest.

"You've got a gorgeous set of sisters there," he muttered, then suddenly clutched the center of her bra and ripped it apart.

Though she let out a startled gasp, she raised her chest, begging for attention. Pushing the torn garment aside, he lowered his lips and devoured her nipples, diving from one to the other, hungrily sucking each in turn.

"Fuck me?" she begged. "Please, Connor, I want you so badly."

To her great joy, he rested his weight on top of her, pushed her legs apart with his own, then stretched across to his nightstand, opened the drawer and retrieved a condom.

"I wasn't sure I had one," he mumbled, ripping open the packet.

"Thank God. You would have had a crazy woman on your hands."

"No," he said with a smile as he sheathed himself. "I would've taken care of things."

"I suspect you always find a way to take care of things."

"You got that right. I'm a take-care-of-things sorta guy, and now I'm gonna take care of you."

Clutching her hips, he pulled her pelvis into his, placed himself at the entrance of her hungry, soaked channel, and slowly pushed forward.

* * *

April's grateful moan sent his eyes across her body, and as he began to thrust, he noticed her fingers were gripping the bedspread.

"You okay, darlin'?"

"Ooh, Connor, I've never been more okay in my whole life," she mewled, closing her eyes. "You feel heavenly."

As he quickened his pace, she began panting, almost as if she was nearing an orgasm, and her eyes squeezed shut. He pumped harder, and she cried out, begging for more, but he denied her, slowing down, afraid their hot, intense chemistry would bring them both to the brink too soon.

"You're consuming me," she suddenly cried. "Don't stop. Please, don't stop."

Her needy plea gripped him, and plunging forward he fucked her with abandon, his hands tight around her hips. His eyes still locked on her body, he gazed lustily at her bouncing tits, then her open mouth as it hailed his name between her loud moans. When she arched her back, then abruptly drew in a breath and held it, he knew it was time.

"Come on, darlin'," he growled. "Give it to me."

With a high-pitched squeal she surrendered to her climax, and as she shuddered and wailed, his cock exploded, sending sweeping convulsions through his body. He could hear her ongoing cries through his guttural groans, and when she let out a breathless yowl and fell limp, the last of his spasms waned, and his cock slipped from her depths. Falling beside her, his heart pumping wildly, he moved his arms around her.

Together they drifted...

"May I ask you something?" she whispered, coming out of her serene state.

Stirring from his doze, he opened his eyes.

"Anything."

"Your first thought, right now."

He stared up at the ceiling, then slowly shifting on to his side he stared down at her.

"A song."

"Really?"

"We Danced. Brad Paisley."

"Ooh, Connor, I love that song."

"I'd be sweepin' the floor ready to close up, wishin' you'd walk in, and I'd put the dang thing on my CD and torture myself."

"That is so weird," she said softly. "Whenever I heard it on the radio I'd think about you. I mean, you were always in the back of my mind, but when I'd hear that song, I could see us alone in your tavern dancing."

"April, I think we've found somethin' mighty special."

"We have, and it's our very own Christmas miracle."

* * *

As they crawled under the covers for a much needed nap, Connor closed his eyes and breathed her in, thinking back to the many nights he'd prayed she'd walk through his door. Though her arrival had been alarming, he didn't care. His instincts had been right. She was everything he'd expected her to be. Swept up by a yawn, he let himself drift away, but in the back of his mind he knew there was more drama to come...

CHAPTER SEVEN

Connor woke first. Glancing at the clock, the glowing blue digits told him it was almost one-o'clock. It would soon be time to leave. A soft smile curled his lips. He'd baked a delicious rum-laced yellow cake, and gifts were in cartons waiting to be loaded into the car. Though blown away by the sudden turn of events, they validated his belief being with April was meant to be.

Slipping softly from the bed, he padded across the room and looked out his window. Suzy was a Godsend. He'd texted the night before to let her know he wouldn't be home. Mitch and Molly were out of the barn, blanketed and pawing at the snow. Looking past them, his neighbor's sprawling acreage sat behind a fence a few yards beyond the stable. A former horse facility, it had a twelve-stall barn in good condition, a covered arena, several fenced paddocks, and while the outdoor riding ring needed cleaning up, it was nothing he couldn't manage with the tractor.

His successful tavern carried value. As much as he was loathe to give it up, the money from the sale would finance the purchase of the land and improvements. His neighbor had said he would probably put his property on the market at the beginning of the year. That was just around the corner. Though land didn't sell fast, especially in the middle of winter, finding the right buyer for the tavern would also take a while. Not wanting a bridge loan, or the weight of carrying two properties, his dream depended on the right people stepping up at the right time.

"You brought April into my life," he murmured, "and I thank you from the bottom of my heart. Please open the door to my ranch."

"Who are you talking to?"

Turning around, he found April wide awake and propped up on an elbow.

"The Christmas fairy," he replied with a grin, ambling back to the bed.

"You believe in the Christmas fairy?" she said with a giggle. "A macho man like you?"

"Hey, she brought you into my life, didn't she?"

"Maybe it was the Good Lord."

"Maybe it was. Regardless, I just asked for help with my future plans."

"You mean buying the land and building your ranch?"

"Yep, and speakin' of ranches, tell me what it is you do? Are you a trainer?"

"Nope. I'm a horse appraiser."

"You're a what?"

"A horse appraiser, as in, I appraise horses."

"I didn't even know there was such a thing. How did you get into it?"

"I've wanted horses as a career, but training didn't appeal to me, and I wasn't good enough to be a professional rider, then one day an appraiser came to my barn. It was fascinating. The more I watched him, the more I knew it was for me."

"Damn. April, I need you. My ranch will be breedin' and sales, Mitch and Molly have taught me retired horses have a lot to offer, and I will bring in more, along with some rescues, but when it comes to findin' good dams and sires, I sure could use your expertise."

"You just gave me goosebumps," she exclaimed, stretching out her arm.

"This is all kinds of weird," he muttered, staring at her bumpy skin. "How do you go about it?"

"I take into account bloodlines, conformation, soundness, temperament, the horse's success if it's a show horse, things like that. It's a bit like real estate. What are similar horses selling for? It takes research, and my services don't come cheap, but it's worth it if a buyer is spending a lot of money."

"I am seriously impressed. Did you do any actual work for the Churchill's?"

"I finished two appraisals, and when I came back I started on two more. They have some really nice horses, and I have to say, they're extremely well cared for."

"Do they owe you any money?"

"Uh-huh, but no way will I go after it. If I never see them again it will be too soon."

"They rarely come into this town, which is just as well," he remarked, lowering his voice. "I'm gonna make sure you'll be spendin' a lotta time here."

"That works for me, cowboy," she purred, moving her arms around his neck.

"We should probably make a move. I need to shower and change, but you don't have any other clothes."

"No, I don't," she muttered, a frown crossing her face, "and with the shops closed I won't be able to pick anything up until tomorrow."

"Or maybe the day after, this is a sleepy town, but I have no objection if you want to run around naked."

"Surprise, surprise!"

"Sassy!"

"That would be me," she replied with a laugh. "Ah, well, I'll survive, but could I borrow a sweatshirt when we get back? I'd like to wash my sweater."

"No problem. You looked great in my pajama top."

"Shoot, I just had a thought. I need to repair my bra. I don't fancy being at your friend's house on high-beam. Would you happen to have a needle and thread in this house?"

"Yeah, but I hate to let you use it."

"You're incorrigible."

"I can't help it," he said with a wink, rolling on top of her and devouring her neck, but abruptly pulled back. "Damn, you drive me crazy, woman. Enough! I'd better check on the tavern before I jump in the shower."

"I don't understand?"

"I have security cameras," he said, sitting up and grabbing the television remote control from the nightstand.

"I didn't see any signs."

"I don't want any signs," he replied, turning on the set. "I had them up for a while, but they're obnoxious. People come to the tavern to relax. They don't need to be reminded they're on film."

"Good point," she said as he flipped through the channels.

"There's the parking lot."

"Oh, wow. That's so cool. Hey, am I on film?"

"You are, and I confess, after you left, I looked at it over and over again."

"Aw, Connor, that's so sweet."

"Please, I'm a guy," he grunted, shooting her a look.

"Yeah, but you're a sweet guy."

"If you say so," he said, switching to the inside of the tavern. "Up here I only have this television, but downstairs in my office I have monitors so I can watch several locations at once."

"How much fun is this? I love it."

Studying the bar area and the kitchen, and finding everything as it should be, he turned to the local news station.

"I'm gonna jump in the shower," he declared, handing her the remote. "I'd invite you to join me, but if I do we'll never get outta here."

"You've got that right," she retorted with a giggle.

"Hey, April. I just had a thought. That mall in Clearview will be open tomorrow, and they'll have after-Christmas sales."

"Except...I don't want to run into the Churchill's."

"It's a big place, and I'll be with you. Trust me, if they see my face they'll run the other way."

"My hero."

"All in the line of duty, ma'am. I won't be long."

*　*　*

Watching him disappear into the bathroom, April sighed happily, then idly humming, *We Danced*, she settled back against the headboard to watch the news. Connor was everything she'd imagined, and though she didn't want to get ahead of herself, she began to imagine the life they could share. She was still day-dreaming when she heard the shower turn off.

"But what will we do in the meantime?" she muttered, watching television but not really paying attention. "I live five hours away. A day at a time, I guess. If it's meant to be—oh, shit," she suddenly exclaimed, seeing her face alongside the report of a stolen car. "Connor! Connor! Come quick!"

"What is it?" he asked urgently, hurrying through the bathroom door with a towel around his waist.

"I'm a wanted woman," she exclaimed, panic-stricken. "What am I going to do?"

"Hey, easy there," he said, keeping his voice calm as he strode forward. "What are you talkin' about?"

"My picture and name, it was on TV. The reporter said I'm wanted for stealing a car, and I'm unstable and dangerous. The Churchill's must have called the sheriff."

"Dangerous?"

"Yes, he said if anyone sees me, not to approach and call the sheriff."

"Those bastards," Connor growled. "Becky, the waitress at the diner, she's a sweetheart and a friend of mine, but if she saw that news report..."

As if on cue his cellphone rang. Hurrying to pick it up, he frowned as he looked at the screen.

"Speak of the devil," he grunted, accepting the call. "Hey, Becky, what's up?"

"Connor, have you seen the news?"

"Why?"

"That girl you were with, she stole a car and she's wanted by the police. You should call them."

* * *

Connor paused.

He didn't want Becky to lie for him, and he didn't want to lie to her, but he had to protect April.

"Becky, you know I'm a good guy, right?"

"Are you kidding? You're the best."

"I'm gonna tell you the truth. The girl on the TV, the girl you saw with me, is not unbalanced and she didn't steal a car, not technically. Do you know the Churchill's?"

"Of course."

"She was at their house and had to get out in a hurry."

"I'm not surprised to hear that," Becky said solemnly. "They're strange. Two of the brothers were in the diner today the same time you were. Hey, I remember now, you were talking to one of them."

"Yep, and I'm sorry, Becky, I can't go into details, but believe me when I tell you, April did nothin' wrong. If the police swing by, and there's a good chance they will, I don't want you to lie. I would never put you in that position."

"I'll only tell them I saw you together," she said firmly. "I won't call them. If you say she's cool, then she's cool."

"You're a doll."

"No problem, and if you see her, tell her I hope everything works out."

"Thanks, hon. I'll speak to you later."

Ending the call, he looked up and saw April sitting anxiously on the edge of the bed.

"Connor! If she saw us, so did a bunch of other people. The police will come here, slap me in handcuffs and take me away," she exclaimed. "Shit. What am I going to do?"

"First off, if anyone's gonna slap any handcuffs on you, it's gonna be me," he said with a wink, hoping some levity would help.

She stared back at him, her lips curling in a weak smile.

"Everything will be fine," he continued, sitting next to her and putting his arm around her shoulders. "You texted Richard and told him where the car was, so how can they say it was stolen?"

"Oh, my gosh, that's right."

"We'll go to Lance's and have a nice time, then I'll call Wes Baxter. He's the sheriff and a friend of mine. We'll sort this out, but after we've had a real happy Christmas. Got it?"

She nodded her head, then leaned into his arms.

"Please tell me again everything will be okay."

"I promise it will. Remember what I said? I'm a take-care-of-things kinda guy, and I'll take care of this."

"I do believe you, but I hope the Churchill's clout doesn't—"

"Hey, we've got Christmas magic on our side," he said softly, cutting her off. "Think about all the crazy things that have brought us together. It's not about to fall apart now."

"Thank you for saying that," she said with a sigh. "We do have something amazing happening. I just have to keep the faith."

"I would suggest we leave for Lance's quickly though. Wes could show up, and I don't want to be late. I also want to reach out to him before he comes lookin' for me."

CHAPTER EIGHT

Though April wanted to meet Mitch and Molly, Connor didn't want to loiter. As he hurriedly loaded up his SUV and pulled out of the garage, she sensed his relief. Speeding away from the house, she suddenly felt the same. There was no doubt the sheriff would come knocking. She just hoped Connor's word carried weight, and the sheriff would believe her story. The fact that she was a stranger in town probably wouldn't help. It was only a ten minute drive to Lance's ranch, and as they turned up his driveway, she gazed at horses frolicking in the snow.

"What a gorgeous sight," she said happily. "Every time I'm in a rural area like this it feeds my soul. I'm so tired of the city."

"I couldn't live anywhere else," Connor remarked. "I don't know why a country boy like me was born into noisy traffic and steel mountains. At least I was able to get out."

"Don't you miss your family?"

"Sure, but I visit a lot, and they love comin' out here," he replied, then looked up and grinned. "Here comes the welcoming committee."

A herd of dogs bounded towards them, and as Connor slowed down, they began barking and running around his Jeep.

"Oh, my, gosh, how many are there?" April exclaimed, laughing out loud.

"Too many," Connor replied with a grin, "and the kids are gettin' a puppy today."

"Good grief. Why?"

"Because the oldest is gettin' her first pony. It's a consolation prize for the younger two, but it's a lap dog, unlike these other delinquents."

"That poor puppy, he'll get eaten alive," she continued, watching a large hound gallop to the front door barking furiously. "This begs the question, why don't you have a dog?"

"I want one, but I have to be at the bar all the time. The minute I'm outta there, my first stop will be the animal shelter."

"I hope I'm here when you go."

"I'll make sure you are," he said, rolling to a stop, then to her delight, he leaned over and lightly kissed her. "That's a promise."

Climbing from the car, and immediately surrounded by the happy dogs, the morning's news report fell to the back of her mind. A moment later the front door opened, and a burly cowboy wearing a Santa hat and a bright red sweater started walking towards them.

"Merry Christmas you two!" he said cheerily as he approached, the canines leaping around him. "You must be April. Good to meet you. I'm Lance."

April liked him immediately. He radiated joy, and his brown eyes were warm and welcoming.

"Hi Lance, it's great to meet you as well. This is an amazing place you have here, and what a wonderful bunch of pooches."

"I'd tell you their names, but I'm not sure I can remember them all," he said with a laugh. "Don't tell the kids though. They'll never forgive me."

"Can you give me a hand?" Connor asked, trying to pull a carton of gifts from the back seat, but having a tough time surrounded by the buoyant bevy of hyper animals.

"Uncle Connor! Uncle Connor!"

Three excited children suddenly raced down the front steps, the oldest introducing herself as Izzy. Taking April's hand, she led her to the house, chattering about what she was expecting from Santa Claus. Walking through the door, April was greeted by the inviting smell of cinnamon and coffee, and glancing in the large living room, she spied a decorated tree loaded with gifts.

"I thought you had only one brother and one sister," she said as Izzy dragged her towards it.

"That's right," the little girl answered. "Why do you think I have more?"

"All those presents can't possibly be for just three children."

As Izzy started giggling, her mother appeared from the kitchen wiping her hands with a towel.

"Hi, April, I'm Annabelle. I hope it's not too crazy for you. We're a bit of a wild bunch, especially at Christmas time."

"Not at all, I think it's wonderful."

"Can I get you some eggnog, coffee? What would you like?"

"Whatever you have that's easy," April replied. "Can I help? Is there anything I can do?"

"Everything is under control. Izzy here is an excellent assistant, and we did most of it last night, right, Izzy?"

"Uh-huh, and I made the dressing. It's really good."

"But you're welcome to come back to the kitchen. I'm just finishing up some bits and pieces."

"Sure," April replied as Connor and Lance lumbered through the door carrying the cartons. "Connor, I'm just going into the kitchen," she called as he began unloading the presents.

"Okay," he called back, but as she disappeared, he quickly turned to Lance. "I need to talk to you. I have a big problem on my hands."

* * *

Not wanting to be heard from the kitchen, Connor and Lance walked across the room and stood by the bay window.

"What's up?" Lance asked quietly.

"Those dang Churchill's told the sheriff April stole a car and is mentally unstable. It was on the news. They're lookin' for her."

"That sounds like the Churchill's," Lance muttered, shaking his head. "I'm surprised they haven't pressed charges against you as well."

"I made sure there was no-one around when I took them down."

"Just as well," Lance said solemnly. "Wes will have to talk to April. It's his job. Mind you, it's Christmas day. He might wait until tomorrow."

But their conversation was cut short as Annabelle and Izzy appeared with eggnog and plates of bite-sized morsels.

"Let's sit down," Annabelle said, placing the jug and plates on the coffee table. "What's been happening with you, Connor?"

As they settled in to enjoy the appetizers, Connor could see April was beginning to relax. The atmosphere was happy and comfortable, until the dogs outside suddenly barked up a storm.

"Are you expectin' anyone, hon?" Lance asked, rising to his feet and walking to the door.

"Not that I recall."

"It's the sheriff," Lance said quietly, spying the blue and white car through the window.

"Come on, kids," Annabelle said, quickly rising to her feet. "We need to go back to the kitchen and put our wonderful dinner into the serving dishes."

"I can't wait," Izzy exclaimed, jumping up and following her mother, along with her brother and sister.

Connor's heart skipped a beat.

Glancing at April, he saw fear in her eyes.

"I'd better see what he wants," Lance continued, striding across the room and opening the front door. "Hey, Wes, what brings you out this way? Come on in."

"I figured Connor would be joinin' you, and I hate to interrupt—"

But seeing April in the living room, he stopped speaking and walked forward.

"Hello, Wes," Connor said, keeping his voice measured as he stood up. "I know why you're here. I saw the news, and it was dead wrong."

"Wouldn't be the first time," Wes declared, "but I'm obliged to find out. Young lady, are you April Sullivan?"

"I am."

"I'm Sheriff Wes Baxter, and I'm sorry to do this on Christmas day, but I've gotta take you down to the station and ask you some questions."

"Because?"

"You've been accused of stealin' a car and attackin' Edward Churchill in his home."

"What kind of attack?" Connor asked.

"First, the car was found in a ditch not far from your bar, and they say she took a bronze statue and smashed it into Edward Churchill's nose. They've got the bronze with the blood on it, and Edward's a mess. Will we find your prints on that bronze, April?" he finished, turning to face her.

"Wes, it wasn't April," Connor said hastily, "it was me who—"

"Yes, my prints will be on that bronze," April interjected, jumping to her feet.

"What are you sayin'?" Connor demanded, spinning around and glaring at her.

"Daddy, what's going on?"

But Izzy's voice brought the conversation to a screeching halt.

"I'd like the answer to that question myself," Annabelle declared, walking up behind her daughter.

"We've got a bit of a situation," Wes replied, softening his voice. "I'm gonna have to take April back to the station with me so we can talk privately."

"You can talk privately here," Izzy insisted. "When mommy and daddy say they have to talk privately, they go into their room and close the door. You can do that, can't he mommy? I don't want April to leave. I want her here for Christmas. I even have a present for her."

A heavy frown crossed the sheriff's face.

Connor could see the man was torn.

"Wes, may I speak with you outside for a moment?" Connor asked.

"Why don't you do that, sheriff?" Annabelle said firmly, and though she was smiling, her eyes made it clear she'd have no more discussion in the house.

"Sure," Wes agreed, starting for the door. "Let's go Connor."

"I'm coming with you," April declared.

"Stay here," Connor retorted, shooting her a look.

"Yes, you stay here, April," Izzy piped up. "Come into the kitchen and help mommy and me."

"All right, Izzy," April said, taking her hand. "Show me what needs to be done."

"I'm joinin' you two," Lance said, following Connor and Wes outside to the porch.

"I need to sit a spell," the sheriff muttered, settling into a deck chair. "Okay, Connor, let's hear what you have to say."

"This all started about a month ago," Connor began.

As he relayed the full story, Wes listened attentively, then studied the texts between April and Richard regarding the whereabouts of the car.

"Huh," Wes grunted, "that's a pretty far-fetched story, Connor. You're accusin' the Churchill's of holdin' April against her will. That's pretty darn serious."

"I wasn't there, but I know how desperate she was when I found her, and I don't think anyone would struggle through a snowstorm the way she did unless they feared for their life. Do you?"

"I can't say I do."

"There's more," Connor declared. "When you view my security cameras, you'll see the terrible state she was in for yourself. You'll hear the fear in her voice. You'll also see the Churchill's bangin' on my door, and if one of them was Edward, he sure as heck won't be sportin' a broken nose. You can also talk to Becky at the diner. She'll tell you he was fine when he was there this mornin'. I'm surprised he forgot he'd been seen."

"You've given me a lot to chew on," Wes said with a frown, "though April claims she did what they say, but if she hasn't been back to the Chateau, and your video and Becky confirm he was okay this mornin', that changes everything."

"She hasn't been back there," Connor insisted. "She's been with me every moment since I found her on my floor, but she was stayin' at the Chateau, so of course her prints will be there."

"I've got the picture," Wes said holding up his hand. "I know your word is good, and she doesn't strike me as a girl who would go around bonkin' folks on the nose, but that's off the record. You, on the other hand..."

"I told you, I had to defend myself and protect her. They were harassing her, and jumped me."

"I want you and April at the station around 10 a.m. Bring your evidence and we'll get this thing sorted out."

"Thanks, Wes," Lance said gratefully. "I don't think Izzy would have forgiven you if you'd taken April away."

"That little girl is somethin' else," the police chief remarked, rising to his feet. "All right fellas, you have a Merry Christmas."

Watching the sheriff march to his car and drive away, Lance shook his head and let out a grunt.

"Connor, this is a mess. Those Churchill's can be mean. They may not let this go."

"I'm not scared of them, besides, April and I have the truth on our side, and the evidence to back it up."

"That's not what I'm worried about," Lance said solemnly. "You need to watch your back."

"Yeah, okay, but I also need to have a quiet word with my girl."

"You want me to send her out here?"

"Would you mind?"

"As long as you don't take too long. Annabelle's about to serve dinner."

"Just a couple of minutes."

"Okay, but no more," Lance warned. "She doesn't like her food gettin' cold."

But as he started to move away, April walked out.

"I saw the squad car drive off," she exclaimed. "What happened?"

"I'll leave you to it," Lance said, heading inside and closing the door behind him.

"Connor, I don't know why the sheriff left without me," she began, standing over him, "but I'm going to tell him I hit Edward with that bronze. The only reason you punched him was because of me, so I'm to blame. I won't let you get into trouble for something that's my fault."

"Have you finished?"

"I have. Now I'm going back inside. Are you coming?"

"Hmm, I wonder..." he murmured, tilting his head to the side.

"What?"

"How hard I'll have to spank you when we get home before you see sense."

"What...?"

"You listen to me, little lady," he said sternly, abruptly standing and gripping her arms. "I appreciate you wantin' to keep me outta trouble, but I know how to deal with this, and even if I didn't, do you think, for one, single, solitary second, I'd let you take the blame for somethin' I did? Hell, I'm proud of punchin' those yokels. They've had it comin' for a long time."

"But, Connor—"

"This discussion is over. We're goin' back in that house, we're gonna have a nice time, then we're goin' home, and I'm gonna spank you real good."

"Why?"

"Cos I wanna make sure you're not gonna do or say anythin' stupid when we visit the sheriff in the mornin'."

"We're going in the morning?"

"Yep. You're gonna do exactly what I tell you, and I'm gonna make sure you'll be sittin' on a tender backside so you don't forget. You understand?"

She stared up at him for a moment, then threw her arms around his neck and hugged him.

"You just made my knees weak, and I think I feel a bit faint."

"I'm still gonna spank you."

"You don't have to. I get the message."

"I don't make empty promises, and we're not talkin' about this again until we're home. Got it?"

"Uh-huh, I've got it. I've got everything," she sighed, then looking up at him she added, "and you take my breath away."

CHAPTER NINE

The Christmas meal was so festive, fun and delicious, April almost forgot about the Churchills and the ongoing drama. Though not used to being around young children she found their little minds amazingly imaginative, especially when Izzy explained how Santa's reindeer were able to fly around the globe overnight. According to Izzy, their antlers were like the engines in airplanes, and with so many pulling Santa's sleigh it was able to travel extra fast. The theory remained the topic of conversation until Annabelle produced a flaming cake for dessert.

"It's a British tradition, and it's called a plum pudding," she exclaimed proudly as she placed it on the table. "I'll bring out the ice cream, but I also made English Custard, that's what they pour over it."

Her declaration set off a round of excited chatter about holiday rituals around the world. As the meal finally came to an end, Lance rose to his feet and suggested they visit the horses and treat them to extra carrots.

"Can't we open our presents first?" Izzy asked hopefully, pushing back from the table.

"The horses are waiting. You don't want to disappoint them, do you?" Annabelle asked. "We've had our Christmas dinner. They should have their Christmas carrots."

"Okay," Izzy said with a sigh, "but can we go right now?"

"We can go right now," Lance replied with a chuckle.

As the happy group left the house and started down to the barn, April looped her arm through Connor's.

"I'm so excited to be a part of this," she whispered as they approached. "I can't wait to see Izzy's face."

Though the horses were in their paddocks, Lance had led the group into the stable to pick up the treats, but instead of entering the feed room, he stopped at a stall.

"Izzy, we have a new member of our horse family waiting to meet you," he declared, sliding open the door and stepping inside. Leading out the adorable dark bay pony, he walked up to Izzy and handed her the lead rope. "His name is Cocoa, and he's all yours."

Izzy was so thrilled, she stood completely speechless with her mouth open and her eyes bulging, then utterly overcome, she burst into tears and wrapped her arms around the pony's neck.

"I love him, I love him," she exclaimed. "Thank you. Thank you."

Watching the joyful scene unfold, April found herself swallowing back a lump in her throat.

A shiver pricked her skin.

She was witnessing the life she wanted.

* * *

A little while later when they returned to the house, the new puppy was brought into the room and created hysterical havoc. Leaping from box to box and racing around the presents, the puppy thought it was a great game and led everyone on a merry Christmas chase. The bedlam continued non-stop, with Annabelle and Lance finally giving up control and letting the mayhem reign.

The kids and puppy finally ran out of steam, and Connor and April said their goodbyes. Carrying their gifts, they ambled out to the car and found the early evening clear and chilly. Driving home, April leaned across the console trying to cuddle against him.

"What a wonderful day," she said with a happy sigh. "I'll never forget it. Those kids are incredible, but I'm not surprised with parents like Lance and Annabelle. They're such lovely people."

"Yep, it was a great day, even with Wes arrivin' on the doorstep."

"Can you please tell me why you think my big mess is going to be okay? I don't see how, and we can debate it all you want, but I'm determined you're not going to be arrested for punching that creepy Edward."

"Didn't we have this conversation?"

"I guess, but you still haven't answered my question. What did you mean when you said you knew how to handle it?"

"You know I have camera's around the bar, inside and out. It's easy to prove Edward was fine last night, and that you've been with me ever since you collapsed on my floor."

"Of course! The security cameras!"

"I've already shown Wes the texts you exchanged with Richard. When he sees the videos—case closed."

"But what about me stealing the car? In those texts I admit I took it."

"If those texts prove anything, it would be you had to take the car to run for your life," Connor declared, "and you used the word borrowed. I'm surprised the Churchill's forgot about that, though I suppose it's possible Richard didn't tell them."

"Or remembered too late," April suggested. "I bet that's what happened, but you're right, and the security cameras will show how desperate I was. What a relief."

"Silly girl—about to confess to something that's so easy to disprove."

"I panicked, but I'd happily take the blame for Edward's busted nose. This is all my fault."

"Dammit, April, it's not your fault, and it's not my fault. The crazy Churchill clan is to blame for all this crap."

With the heater taking the chill from the car, and reassured the nightmare was about to end, she sat back in her seat and thought about the days ahead.

She had commitments.

She had to get back to the city, and soon.

It was the last thing she wanted to do.

"It was so kind of Annabelle to lend me a few things to tide me over," she remarked. "I wish I could get my things from the chateau, but I can't go back there. But at least I can go shopping tomorrow."

"April, look at that moon," Connor exclaimed. "Have you ever seen anything like it?"

Gazing through the windshield, April stared up at the huge white and grey globe hanging low in the sky.

"Oh, my, gosh, I've never seen it so big. It's gorgeous. Why didn't we see it at the ranch?"

"It's so low it would have been hidden behind the trees."

"Um, Lance, isn't your house in the other direction?"

"Yep."

"Where are we going?"

"Back to the tavern."

"May I ask why?"

"You can ask, but I'm not about to tell you. It's a surprise."

"I didn't think this day could get any better," she murmured softly, "but maybe I'm wrong."

"Maybe you are," he replied, shooting her a wink.

With the enchanting moon lighting their path, Connor continued through the quiet town, turned onto the main road, drove a couple of miles, then swung into the tavern's empty parking area. Rolling to a stop and jumping out, he hurried around to open April's door.

"So gallant," she said with a grin. "Thank you."

"I'm not about to waste a moon like that," he murmured hugging her tightly. "Makes me think of that song, Moondance. I wish I could sing it to you, but you'd run a mile if I tried."

"Never," she said, lifting her eyes and soaking in the extraordinary sight. "It's spellbinding."

"Like you," he whispered, slipping his fingers into her hair, "and this..."

Tugging back her head, he lovingly pressed his lips on hers.

His passion quickly took hold.

Pushing his tongue between her teeth and fervently devouring her mouth, she threw her arms around his neck, clinging with a hungry urgency. Finally breaking apart, he put his arm around her shoulders and moved into the tavern. With nightlights washing the bar in their dim light, he led her to a booth.

"Wait here. I'll be right back."

Her pulse ticking up, she watched him walk behind the bar. Moments later, the slow opening bars of *We Danced,* floated through the room. Her heart soaring as he ambled back to her, she rose to her feet, then leaned into him as he took her in his arms. Weightless as he moved her effortlessly across the floor, the deep soulful voice of the singer seemed to touch her soul.

"That was sheer heaven," she breathed as the classic hit faded away. "I never wanted it to end."

"It's just the beginnin', darlin'," he promised, holding her head in his hands, "and right now I wanna be with you in my big comfortable bed, and if I stay here one more minute we'll be sleepin' upstairs."

"I'd like to sleep in your big comfortable bed as well, but Connor, I'll always remember this moment."

"Me too, and we can relive it whenever we want. It's on camera. Now let's get home and get naked."

"Yes, please."

Arm-in-arm they ambled to the front door, but paused to stare back across the tavern. Committing the magical moment to memory, she stepped outside and gazed up at the perigee moon. The hellish time with the Churchill's almost felt like a bad dream.

"When we get home, it's straight in the shower to wash off the pony and the dogs and the kids," Connor declared as they climbed into his Jeep.

"That sounds like an excellent plan, but I hope you mean together."

"Do you even have to ask?" he quipped, leaning across and giving her a soft kiss.

The drive back to his home was a quick one, and as they rolled into the garage, April felt a wave of weariness. Deciding to leave everything in the car except the clothes Annabelle lent April, they walked in the house, climbed the stairs, with Connor peeling off his clothes on his way into the bathroom. As he reached into the shower to turn on the faucets, April began to undress, but caught him watching her in the reflection from the mirror above the sink. Smiling as she stripped, she turned and sashayed over to him. His arm came around her waist, and he jerked her into his body.

"Just as well we're standin' here with the water runnin', or I'd toss you on my bed in a heartbeat."

"But you can wash me instead."

"Oh, babe, I intend to," he said huskily, bustling her into the shower and pushing her back against the wall.

Grabbing the sponge from the built-in alcove, he dropped in a dollop of gel, rubbed it over her chest and down to her breasts. Closing her eyes, she let out a soft moan, but his fingers suddenly slid between her legs eliciting a surprised cry.

"Such a hungry girl," he purred, circling her clit. "Tell me what you want."

"I want you to take me to bed," she whimpered, wriggling as he continued the tantalizing torment.

"And once I've got you between the sheets...?"

"Please will you make love to me."

"You know what has to come first," he whispered, his lips at her ear as he thrust his fingers into her depths, making her catch her breath. "Tell me, my sweet Christmas angel."

"Ooh, Connor, you have to spank me."

"Tell me why," he insisted, abruptly shoving his fingers in and out of her channel.

"I can't think."

"You don't have to think, naughty girl. You already know the answer. Why do I have to spank you?"

"Because of what I said to the sheriff about hitting Edward with that bronze when I didn't," she bleated breathlessly.

"What else?"

"Uh..."

"When you insisted you would've carried through with your confession, you were testin' me, weren't you, April? The truth."

"Yes, Connor," she whispered, dropping her head into her shoulder. "I don't know why."

Wordlessly dropping his fingers from between her legs, he cupped her backside with one hand, and gripped her damp hair with the other.

"Cos you wanted to make sure of me," he murmured, tugging it back.

"Connor..."

"Hush," he warned, staring at her with a glint in his eye. "You'll be sleepin' real good tonight. I'm gonna turn your ass bright red, then ride you 'til you're screamin'. You'll find out you always sleep better with a toasty backside and a satisfied pussy."

CHAPTER TEN

His voice was low and husky, and his promise sent a warm thrill rippling through her body. Abruptly dropping on her knees, she began lustily sliding her tongue up and down his stiffening shaft, then took him into her mouth. His fingers gripped her hair and began controlling her movements, but it was only a few minutes before she heard him groan and made her stop.

"What am I gonna do with you?" he growled, tugging her head back and staring down at her.

"Spank me hard," she rasped gazing up at him. "I've been such a bad girl."

Wordlessly clutching her arms and pulling her to her feet, he hastily turned off the shower, then bustled her back into the bathroom and dried her off. "Be careful what you ask for," he declared, wiping the towel quickly over his body and scooping her up. "You wanna know how it feels?" he continued, carrying her to his bed and throwing her on the mattress, "you're about to."

Positioning her on all fours and kneeling at her side, he wrapped his arm around her waist and delivered a volley of rapid-fire swats.

"Ow, ouch," she yelped, shocked at the speed and severity of his hard, spanking hand.

"Now you'll know what I'm talkin' about if I say you're in for a good spankin.'"

"Enough, stop," she exclaimed, kicking out her legs.

"When I'm spankin' you like this, you call me, Sir."

"Yes, Sir," she said quickly. "Please, Sir, enough."

"You think you can tell me when it's enough?" he demanded, whisking his hand across her sit spot. "You might wanna reconsider that statement."

"Ouch. Okay, I don't know when enough is enough."

To her great relief he suddenly stopped, then leaned across her body and opened the drawer of the nightstand.

Pulling out a condom and quickly sheathing his cock, he positioned himself behind her, clutched her hips, and placed his member at her entrance.

"You want me?" he grunted, his fingers digging into her skin.

"Yes, yes, please," she begged, bucking back at him. "So much..."

Thrusting inside her, he slow-pumped with gusto, his pubic hairs grazing her hot, stinging backside with every stroke, then suddenly quickening his pace, he pounded her pussy, eliciting a long, bleating groan. As her climax began to build, she curled her fingers into a ball and threw back her head.

"Are you close?" he panted, coming to an abrupt halt.

"Yes," she panted.

His cock began to withdraw, then slammed back inside her.

"How close?" he asked, repeating the dramatic thrust.

"V-very," she managed as he plowed back in.

"Drop down on your elbows."

As she followed his instruction, he delivered several hard swats, evoking loud squeals, then moved his hand beneath her and pressed his finger against her clit.

"You're gonna come, and you're gonna come hard," he grunted. "You understand me?"

"Yes, Sir, I—"

But his cock cut her off, vigorously pumping as his finger agitated her clit.

Her orgasm began to build, taking her higher and higher...

Hurtled into the release, she shrieked through the first, shimmering spasm, and as wave after tingling wave sparkled through her, she heard his deep groans...

The convulsions finally faded.

Her body fell limp.

Slipping out, he dropped beside her.

"Wow," she panted, rolling into him.

"It's only gonna get better," he muttered breathlessly.

"How can you be so sure?"

"I feel it," he replied, letting out a long breath. "Sometimes things just feel like they're meant to be."

She smiled, then swept up by a yawn, she snuggled against him. "I'm so tired."

"You need a long sleep," he said softly, reaching for the bedcovers and pulling them over her.

"I'm already on my way..."

* * *

Switching off the bedside lamp, Connor slid back down and glanced out the window. The bright, radiant light of the full moon illuminated the hills in the distance like a street lamp over a house.

Wishing the night before had been just as clear when the Churchill's had banged on his door, he began to wonder about the video. If Edward had been there, it was possible his image would be murky from the flying snow, or even the protective clothing he might have been wearing.

"Shit," Connor grumbled, knowing he wouldn't be able to sleep without checking the footage.

Gently slipping from the bed, he donned his thick robe and slippers, crept from the room, and made his way down the stairs. As he walked into his office and turned on the lights, he decided he may as well make copies for the sheriff while he was there. Opening up a pack of blank CD's, he sat behind the monitors and powered them up.

Though he had eight cameras, and could view them from his phone, he preferred the monitors. They were much larger, and he could watch the eight views simultaneously using a split screen option. He was about to watch the recording from the night before, when he noticed a vehicle in his parking lot.

A black Range Rover.

His heart skipped.

He zoomed in to see the license plate.

There was none.

His stomach churning, he darted his eyes from camera to camera.

The tavern floor and bar were empty, but when he looked into the kitchen, he saw someone standing by the gas stove. Hastily snatching the receiver from his landline and calling 911, he wondered how the intruder gained entry, and why the alarm hadn't alerted him.

A second intruder suddenly came into view.

Richard Churchill.

The lights in the kitchen had been switched on, but he was carrying a candle.

"Police Department, how may I help?"

"This is Connor McBride," he said urgently, continuing to watch the monitor. "Two men have broken into my tavern, McBride's Bar and Grill."

"Connor?"

"Yes ma'am."

"Hey, Connor, it's Sally Matthews. What's goin' on?"

"Mrs. Matthews, I'm watching from my home on my security cameras. Like I said, two intruders at my bar. One of them is Richard Churchill. The other has his back towards me. That's weird…"

"What is?"

"Richard Churchill just put a lit candle on the kitchen island, and they're leaving."

"Connor, is there a gas stove in that kitchen?"

"Yes, yes there is. Oh, no!"

"I'm calling the fire department and sending out a car. Stay on the line."

"Yep, yep, I'll be here."

Looking back at the parking lot, he watched Richard and his accomplice jump into the Range Rover, speed from the parking lot, and take off down the main road.

"Connor?"

"I'm still here Mrs. Matthews. They just left heading east towards town."

"Copy that, I'll let the boys know."

Then it happened.

As he looked back to the kitchen, there was a flash, then nothing. Darting his eyes to the front view of his tavern, he found it engulfed in flames.

His bar had exploded.

* * *

April jolted awake.

The bed was empty.

A chill pricked her skin.

Switching on the bedside lamp, she stared around the bedroom.

Though the heat was on, she shivered as she climbed from the bed.

Seeing Connor's sweater draped over the chair by the window, she hastily pulled it over her head. It fell to mid-thigh, and she had to roll up the sleeves, but it was warm. Slipping her feet into a pair of socks Annabelle had given her, she marched from the room and into the hall.

"Connor?"

There was no reply.

Trotting down the stairs, she was relieved to see the light coming from his study. Hurrying forward and stepping into the room, she found him sitting in front of several monitors, his elbows on his knees, his head in his hands.

"What's happened?" she asked softly, crouching next to him.

"The tavern," he replied shakily, "they blew it up."

"What...?"

As he slowly raised his head, she was shocked to see his face wet with tears.

"Look," he muttered, pointing to a screen showing his bar surrounded by firefighters trying to fight the blaze.

"Oh, my, God."

As she reached out to hug him, he quickly moved his arms around her, held her tightly for a moment, then let out a breath and pulled back.

"I need to get over there."

"Do you know who did it?"

"Yeah, I watched the whole thing as it happened," he replied. "Richard Churchill and some other guy I couldn't see."

"No!"

"I noticed a black Range Rover in the parking lot. When I checked the inside cameras I saw two people in the kitchen, Richard and someone else. Richard put a candle on the kitchen island and they took off. I guess they turned on the gas and left the candle burning far enough away to get out before it blew," he said with a catch in his voice. "I was on the phone with the police when the explosion happened."

"Connor, what can I do?"

"You're doin' it, darlin'," he mumbled, hugging her tightly. "You know what I keep thinkin'?" he said, pulling back and looking at her intently. "What if we'd decided to stay and been sleepin' upstairs?"

"Don't even go there. We weren't. That's what matters."

"I still don't know why the alarm didn't go off."

"You're sure it was on?"

"Absolutely," he said, releasing her and slowly rising to his feet. "They must have disabled it somehow."

"That would have been Richard. He's an electronics nut."

"It doesn't matter, and I don't think it would have stopped them anyway. Once they were in, it would only take them a minute to turn on the gas and leave that candle. Even if the alarm had gone off, they would've been long gone before anyone arrived."

"At least you have the proof to nail them."

"Yeah, I do," he said gravely, "and I'm gonna make sure they rot in prison for a very long time. They may have powerful friends, but I've got the bastards on film. Let's get over there."

CHAPTER ELEVEN

Quickly dressing and bundling up against the cold, Connor and April headed into the garage and climbed into his Jeep, but as he settled behind the wheel, she urgently grabbed his arm.

"Connor, wait, I just had a thought. Why did Richard blow up the tavern? He doesn't even know your name."

"Obviously he must have found out."

"Exactly!"

Connor paused, staring at her, then leaned back and slapped his forehead.

"Shit!"

"After what happened when we left the diner, all he had to do was ask around," she exclaimed. "Once he found out, I bet he figured out I was at the tavern when he banged on the door trying to find me."

"So...what are you getting at?"

"If they know you own the tavern, they probably also know this is your home. What if they're waiting for you to leave so they can torch this house as well? They could be parked on the street watching for you to leave."

"Shit, you could be right, but..."

"But what?"

"Surely they must know the police would question them."

"Why? They don't know about the security cameras, and I guarantee everyone in the Churchill Chateau will say they were home," she said earnestly, then taking a breath, she added, "I bet they've done other horrible things and walked away. I find it hard to believe burning down your bar is their first criminal act."

Connor sucked in a breath.

She was right.

"I'm taking you over to Lance's. It's not safe for you here."

"We can't risk leaving."

"Then I'll call him and ask him to pick you up."

"No, Connor, please, I'll go crazy hanging around and wondering what's going on."

"April, if you're right, and dammit, I hate to say it but I think you are, I have to get you out of danger," he said anxiously. "This house—the tavern, they're insured and replaceable. You're not."

"I'm staying with you. Call your friend the sheriff and tell him what's going on. We can hang out until help arrives."

"You're impossible," he said glaring at her. "Why are you fightin' me on this? Don't you understand I—I—I don't want you in any danger?"

Taking a breath, she stared at him, sensing he'd been about to say something else and changed his mind.

"April, please, be sensible," he continued. "You, more than anyone, know how insane the Churchills are. What if they break in here with guns and drag you back to their compound?"

"Uh...well..." she stammered, trying to think of a retort, "I understand what you're saying, I really do, but I'm sorry, I can't go," she said adamantly, then snatching the remote key from its compartment, she hastily stepped out and slammed the door.

Her heart racing, and watching him through the window, she could see his anger and frustration. Though she suspected he was probably right, and she should stay with Lance and Annabelle until the drama was over, the thought of leaving in the midst of the chaos was too much to contemplate.

"Listen to me," he said patiently, climbing out and slowly walking around to her side of the garage, "I need to—"

"Connor, listen," she snapped, cutting him off and staring at the garage door. "Do you hear that?"

Standing stock still, he followed her gaze.

"That's a car, and it's stopping," he exclaimed. "How the hell did they get through the gates?"

"If they were able to deal with the alarm system at your tavern, they could certainly deal with your little box out there," she remarked, then suddenly caught her breath. "Those are car doors closing," she muttered, hearing the familiar sounds.

"It must be Edward and Richard," he said softly, striding across to join her.

"Do you think they're headed into the house, or have they blocked the garage door to keep us in?"

"Wow, the way your mind works is something else," he murmured. "I have no idea, but I'm calling Wes."

"Why not 911?"

"I don't know what those lunatic Churchills might do if they hear sirens. Wes will know how to handle this. I sure hope his number is still in my phone."

"He gave you his home number?"

"Yeah, when I was havin' some trouble with a biker gang a while back. Great, here it is."

"Are all the doors and windows locked?" she asked as he placed the call. "Does the house have an alarm?"

"No alarm, but yeah, everything's locked up. The back door has a glass window though."

"I've never understood why doors have windows in them," she said testily. "I mean, what's the point? Break it and you're in."

"I have a shotgun and a pistol, but they're upstairs. Maybe I should try to get up there. Hang on, he just picked up. Wes? Hi, it's Connor."

* * *

Wes had been sleeping soundly when his phone woke him up. With an irritated grunt he'd reached for the receiver, squinting groggily as he'd looked at the tiny screen announcing the caller. Seeing Connor's name, he'd immediately answered.

"Hey, Connor, are you all right?"

"Wes, I've got a big problem. Richard and Edward Churchill broke into my tavern and blew it up."

"Say, what...?" Wes exclaimed, sitting up and switching on the bedside lamp.

"I was about to head over there, but a car just stopped outside my garage door. I think it's them. They must have messed with the entry box at the gates. What should I do?"

"Nothin'. Lock yourselves in and wait. I'm on my way."

While Connor had been on the phone, April had crept across to the door that led into the house. Listening intently and hearing nothing, she cracked it open just as he ended the call.

Her heart leapt.

Edward and Richard were standing in the hall staring into the kitchen. Edward sported a wide bandage across his nose, and Richard seemed agitated. Though she couldn't hear him, he waved his hands in the air as he spoke, then abruptly turned and headed to the staircase.

"April, what are you doin'?" Connor demanded in a hushed whisper as he hurried across to her. "Get away from there."

"Edward's at the end of the hall, and Richard's just gone upstairs," she breathed, silently closing the door and turning around. "Edward has a big bandage across his nose."

"I'm surprised he's here. It has to hurt like hell."

"I guess his pride is hurting him more."

"Or he's followin' orders," Connor said with a frown. "Wes and some deputies will be here shortly."

"Do we have time to wait ? What if that bastard is upstairs setting fire to your bedroom right now?"

"Shit."

"Hang on, I have an idea," she said, spying a fire extinguisher on the wall.

Hurrying over to it, she lifted it off its holder and raised the hose.

"Do you know how to use that thing?" Connor asked with a worried frown.

"The fire department stopped by a barn where I was boarding during a red flag alert to check on things. He taught everyone who happened to be there, so yeah, I do."

"What's your idea?"

"I'll kick the door, and when Edward comes running in I'll blast him."

"That's crazy," Connor said shaking his head. "He could have a weapon."

"We have to do something. They're fucking pyromaniacs."

He paused.

"You're right, but forget about the fire extinguisher. I can knock that joker out in a heartbeat. You kick, then get out of the way and duck down. When he comes in I'll jump him from behind."

"Are you sure? I mean, I can spray him, no problem."

"I'm sure. Put that thing down and kick," he said, hastily standing with his back against the wall beside the door.

Placing the extinguisher on the ground, her heart thumping, she stepped forward and stood ready.

"Now?"

"Yeah, do it!"

Taking a breath, she slammed her foot against the solid wood, then hurried away and bent down.

Seconds ticked by.

Stomping feet drew near.

Her eyes fell on the handle.

It turned.

Adrenalin coursed through her veins as she watched the door begin to slowly move—but Connor yanked it open.

Caught off guard, Edward let out a cry and stumbled forward. Grabbing him from behind, Connor spun him around, punched his gut, then landed a right hook to his jaw. As he fell to the ground, April hurriedly closed the door, then watched Connor drag the groaning young man to the opposite side of the garage.

"I'm going to make sure you can't cause any more trouble," Connor muttered, grabbing a roll of duct tape off the work bench and swiftly wrapping it around Edward's wrists and ankles.

"You did that so fast," April declared as Connor stood up.

"You should see me rope a calf," he panted, straightening up. "Shit—April—behind you—Richard—at the door," but as Connor tried to run to her aid, he tripped over Edward.

Spinning around, she saw Richard striding towards her. Diving for the fire extinguisher, she heaved it up, and with a high-pitched scream she sprayed directly into his face as he lunged forward.

"You fucking bitch," he wailed, his arms flailing. "I'm going to fucking kill you."

"The hell you are," Connor shouted, now on his feet and racing towards them, but Richard's hands had found her throat.

With a mammoth effort, she managed to slam the heavy metal canister into his gut. With a howl of shock and pain, he staggered backwards into Connor, who shoved him on the floor, then hastily fetched the tape and wrapped it around his ankles and wrists.

"You can let that go now, hon," Connor said softly, stepping up to April and prying the heavy canister from her fingers. "Are you okay?"

"I'm not sure," she panted. "I feel shaky."

Quickly resting the extinguisher against the wall, he hugged her tightly, then walked her into the hallway, closing and locking the door behind them.

"Connor, I think I'm going to faint. I've never done anything like that in my life."

"You were unbelievable," he declared, his arm around her shoulders as he guided her into the dark living room and sat her on the couch.

"You scared the crap outta me, but you were incredible. They're done for. You can catch your breath and rest easy."

"What happens now? What about the rest of those lunatics?"

"That's a good question," he replied quietly, letting out a sigh as he pulled her back into his arms. "To be honest, I'm not sure. I think we just opened up one hell of a hornet's nest, but it won't be us runnin' for cover."

CHAPTER TWELVE

The shrill, unexpected ringing of the landline pierced the quiet.

April jumped.

"It's just the phone, darlin'," Connor said hastily.

"Sorry, I guess I'm still edgy," she muttered, leaning into his chest. "You'd better answer it."

"You have nothin' to be sorry for," he said softly, switching on the lamp and picking up the receiver. "Hello?"

"Connor, it's Wes. Are you two okay? I'm out front and I can see the Range Rover in the driveway."

"We're fine, but the culprits aren't lookin' so bright. They're in the garage wrapped in duct tape."

"The Churchill brothers I assume?"

"Yep."

"We're comin' in."

"Great, thanks. I'll open the front door," Connor said, hanging up the phone. "The cavalry is here, hon. This will soon be over."

"Thank, God. Do you have any idea how Richard and Edward got in the house?"

"I'm guessin' the window on the back door," he replied with a frown. "You're right about that. It makes no sense."

"I'm so sorry about your tavern," she mumbled, tears escaping in spite of her best efforts to keep them at bay. "I wish I could do something."

"Hey, it's fine, I'm insured."

As headlights shone through the windows, Connor kissed her on the cheek and started to stand up, but she grabbed his hand.

"Connor, I just thought of something."

"Again? You do that a lot."

"What happened to the tavern is awful, but Richard has done you a huge favor. You won't have to worry about selling it to buy your neighbor's land. The insurance will pay for it."

"Damn, you're right," he muttered. "I guess I was so upset it didn't hit me."

"That's what I call a silver lining."

"Or the answer to a prayer," he murmured as the doorbell echoed through the house. "I'll be right back."

Striding to the front door, he opened it up to find Wes and a slew of deputies behind him.

"Howdy, Connor," Wes said solemnly. "Real sorry to hear about your bar. You've had a helluva night."

"No kiddin', come on in," Connor replied, leading him and his men into the living room.

"My deputies will get the Churchill boys outta here, but we'll have to cordon off the garage and other areas of the house where they might have been. Point me in the right direction."

"Yeah, sure, I figured. Go through to the hall," Connor replied, pointing across the room, "turn right, and it's the first door on the left. The button to open the garage is on the wall next to the light switch."

"Interesting house plan."

"Yeah, I know. When I remodeled this place, I wanted to add an office, and that was the concession. The garage openin' into the hall, not the kitchen."

"Compromise, the secret to happiness, or so my wife keeps tellin' me," the sheriff said with a roll of his eyes. "Okay, boys, you know what to do," he continued, waving his deputies forward. "Go through to the hall, turn right, first door on the left. Read 'em their rights and get 'em in the cars."

As the deputies trooped past, Wes walked around the couch and sat next to April.

"Hey, there, April, how are you?"

"Okay I guess, except I can't stop shaking."

"Connor, you got any decent alcohol in this place?"

"Of course I do, I own a tavern—or rather, I did."

"Sorry," Wes said grimly, shaking his head. "That was thoughtless."

"Hey, I made the joke," Connor replied. "I have pretty much everything. Brandy, whiskey, vodka, beer, what can I get you?"

"It's not for me, it's for your girl here. She needs a little somethin' to take the edge off. What strikes your fancy, April?"

"I'm not sure. Brandy I suppose."

"What about you, Wes?" Connor asked, moving to a drinks cabinet in the corner of the room.

"I'm on duty, thanks anyway, but you should pour yourself a glass as well. Sally Matthews told me you saw what happened. Damn, Connor, that's a lot to take in."

"Yeah, it was—it still is," Connor said grimly, splashing the amber liquor in two glasses. "I couldn't believe what I was seein'. It was like watchin' a movie, except it was real."

"You sure were lucky you turned on those monitors when you did. Who knows when that fire would've been called in if you hadn't."

"Part of my security system is an alarm connected to the fire house. Seeing Richard there, that's the lucky part," Connor said, carrying the glasses back to the couch and handing one to April. "Here you go, darlin.'"

"You drink that," Wes said firmly. "You need to warm your insides and relax a bit."

"I'm fine, really," she murmured, but taking a sip of the soothing liquor, her fingers trembled.

"Your official statements can wait until mornin'," Wes declared, rising to his feet and pulling a notepad and pen from his pocket, "but can you give me a quick rundown?"

"April is the star," Connor said, taking the sheriff's place on the couch next to her. "We were in the garage about to race over to the tavern when she realized Richard Churchill must have found out who I was. When she suggested he could be on his way to set fire to this house as well, it made all kinds of sense. That's when we heard him drive up."

April sat quietly as Connor continued to tell the story, and when he described how she had plunged the fire extinguisher into Richard's stomach, Wes let out a low whistle.

"No wonder you're white as a sheet. I don't like citizens takin' down intruders, but it sounds like you two had no choice, and April, what you did, that took some guts. Connor told me what happened at the Churchill Chateau, and your escape through that snowstorm. It sounds like you've been fightin' for your life since the day you got here."

"It does sort of seem that way" she said, her face crinkling. "Actually, I'm starting to feel a bit funny. It must be the brandy."

"More like you're still in shock," Wes remarked solemnly. "You need to get some rest. Maybe take a few days and go off somewhere."

"I agree," Connor said softly. "We both need a break after all this."

"Excuse me, sheriff."

Looking up, Connor saw one of the younger deputies walking in from the hall.

"I called an ambulance. I think Richard Churchill has a couple of broken ribs, and his brother is pretty messed up. He has a broken nose for sure."

"Did you read 'em their rights?"

"Yes, Sir, they're cuffed, but they're still in the garage. We didn't want to move them without the medics checkin' them out first."

"Are they talkin'?"

"No, sir, they just keep askin' us to call their father."

"Have you?"

"No, sir, we thought you'd probably want to do that."

"Yep, I reckon I will," Wes declared. "Let them know I'm takin' care of it, and I'll tell their dad to meet them at the hospital."

"Yes, sir."

"Anything else?"

"No, sir."

"Come down to the station any time tomorrow," Wes said, turning back to Connor as the deputy left the room. "Bring the camera footage and anything else you have. April, when you're feelin' up to it, I need a detailed account of what happened when you were stayin' at the Chateau."

"I'm sure by tomorrow I'll be fine," she said softly. "I bounce back from things pretty quickly."

"You don't need to push it. There's no rush," Wes assured her as headlights beamed through the window. "That's probably the ambulance," he continued, walking swiftly across the room and looking out at the driveway. "Yep, it's them. I won't be needin' to talk to you anymore tonight, so I'll say goodbye. Get some rest, and come in whenever you're ready."

"I'll walk you to the door," Connor said, placing his glass on the coffee table and rising to his feet. "Uh, Wes, how will I get out of here tomorrow? The Rover is blocking the driveway, and you said the garage will be cordoned off."

"The Rover will be hauled away first thing," Wes replied as they started to the door. "I'll have the boys tape off the areas they need to preserve, and give you a path to your vehicle so you'll be able to leave."

"Great, thanks. One more thing, can you get word to the fire chief and tell him I'll call tomorrow? I'm not leavin' April, and she's in no condition to go anywhere."

"Yeah, of course. I was about to suggest the same thing. You get her into bed. We won't be here much longer, and I'll be calling Henry Churchill in a few minutes. You won't have any more trouble, but I'm gonna leave a patrol car out front just in case."

"Thanks, Wes, thanks for everything," Connor said gratefully, shaking his hand.

"Just doin' my job, and again, I'm real sorry about all this. Get some sleep."

* * *

Standing in the doorway, watching the sheriff march away bathed in the light of the full moon, Connor was reminded of the magic moment he'd shared with April at the tavern.

Suddenly the only thing that mattered was being with her.

He didn't care they'd only just met.

He didn't care she lived miles away.

He didn't care about the Churchills.

He didn't care about revenge.

Taking a last look at the glowing orb low in the sky, a chill rippled down his spine. The tavern's loss was his gain, brought about by a bizarre set of circumstances that defied logic. Swallowing back a wave of emotion, he hurried back to the living room to find April resting her head on the arm of the sofa. She appeared to be asleep.

"Hey, darlin'," he said softly, tracing his fingertip down the side of her cheek. "I'm takin' you up to bed."

"I feel like I've been hit by a truck," she breathed, looking up with half-lidded eyes, "a big one."

"Do you realize you're still in your coat?"

She frowned.

"So are you."

"I know," he said, helping her to her feet. "Everything happened so fast."

Removing his jacket, and helping her out of her long parka, he quickly scooped her up.

"I can walk."

"I'm sure you can, but you're wiped out, and I don't want you slippin' on the stairs," he replied, carrying her out into the hall.

But he was exhausted too.

Climbing the steps carefully, he gratefully entered the bedroom, laid her down and peeled off her clothes. As she slid under the covers, he hastily undressed and slipped in beside her.

"By the way, Wes is leaving a car in the driveway as a precaution," he murmured as she snuggled beside him. "You can rest easy."

"That's very comforting," she said wearily, then taking a quick breath, she murmured, "Connor, something just occurred to me."

"Not again?"

"Uh-huh. That amazing dance at the tavern...then walking out and seeing the moon...it was so perfect, like it was meant to be."

"The feeling to take you there was so strong," he said thoughtfully. "Looking back, it almost feels like it was a goodbye."

"And a hello to a new beginning."

His epiphany at the door suddenly washed through him.

"Our beginnin'," he breathed, holding her tightly as his throat burned hot.

CHAPTER THIRTEEN

Slowly coming out of a deep sleep, April rolled over to snuggle against Connor, but the bed was empty. Glancing at the clock she was shocked to discover it was a few minutes past eleven. Stretching her arms above her head and letting out a long yawn, she climbed from the sheets, donned his robe draped across a chair, slipped on her socks, and made her way down the stairs.

"Connor?"

"I'm in the kitchen."

Moving quickly down the hall, she walked in to find him at the table closing a manila envelope.

"How are you feelin," he asked, rising to his feet and wrapping her up, "did you sleep well?"

"Like I was hibernating. What time did you get up?"

"Around nine-thirty, and you were dead to the world. Have a seat. I've got the eggs ready to be scrambled."

"That sounds great, I'm starving," she replied, settling into a chair. "Did you eat already?"

"Just some toast. I've been waitin' for you. Coffee?"

"Lord, yes, please. What's in the envelope?"

"CD's of the security camera footage for Wes, and I wrote out my statement," he replied, handing her a steaming mug, and popping two slices of bread in the toaster. "I thought it would save time when we go to the station. I just hope I don't have to do it again on an official form."

"Put your name, address, and date at the top, and below that write, My Account of Events on—then the date and time. Sign it at the bottom, and underneath your signature put, I swear this is true Under Penalty of Perjury."

"How do you know about that?" he asked as he poured the eggs into a fry pan.

"Remember I told you my father's a lawyer? He wanted me to follow in his footsteps. I spent my summers at the office. I've seen more forms than you have drinks."

"That's a lot of forms," he said with a chuckle.

"I think I'll write out mine as well, but I'll do a separate one detailing what I witnessed at the Churchill's and what happened the night I took off."

"Sounds like a plan, but before we see Wes, I have to meet the fire chief at the tavern. He's expecting me around noon."

"Then I'd better get myself together," she declared as he placed the scrambled eggs in front of her.

"Thank you. Wow, you used parsley."

"Parsley and scrambled eggs are like salt and pepper."

"I know, but I'm still getting used to being around a man that cooks so well—among other things," she added with a wink.

"Uh-huh, well dig in, then get yourself showered and dressed. If you make me late I'll have to make use of one of those other things," he warned, winking back.

* * *

Though Connor could see the positive side to the loss of his tavern, it was with a heavy heart he drove down the main road. His regulars had become almost like family, and he'd been looking forward to selling the bar and spending time there as a customer.

But as he turned into the parking lot, he caught his breath.

Except for some broken windows, the front of the tavern looked intact.

"What the hell?" he muttered as he drove forward. "I thought the place had been burned to the ground."

"That's amazing," April remarked. "The damage must have happened in the back."

"I bet there's nothing left of the kitchen."

"I assume that's the fire chief," April said, spying a burly man climbing from a red truck.

"Yep, his name is Judd Taylor. He came in almost every Friday night with his wife."

Driving towards him, Connor came to a stop and climbed from the Jeep, then introduced April.

"Judd, I don't get it," he exclaimed. "I was expecting to see nothing but charred remains."

"Fires can be unpredictable and surprising," the chief said knowingly. "Obviously the kitchen was destroyed, and the explosion blew through the ceiling into the second floor, but the fire burned to the side of the building, not the front. That's why it was spared. Your sprinkler system worked a treat, by the way, and so did your alarm. We were here pretty quick."

"Is it a write-off, Judd?" Connor asked solemnly.

The chief tilted his head to the side.

"That's something you'll have to discuss with your insurance company. I'll get you the full report in the next couple of days, but I'd suggest you place some heavy tarps over the structure until you decide what to do. Would you like me to email you the name of a guy who's quick and good and doesn't cost a fortune?"

"Absolutely, I hadn't thought about that, and we'll be gettin' more weather for sure."

"Do you have any questions?"

"Can I go in?"

"You can poke your head through the door, but I wouldn't advise walkin' around in there, not yet anyway."

"Okay, thanks again. I'll speak to you soon."

"Yep," the chief said with a nod, then lowered his voice. "Marjorie and I sure had some good times there."

"We all did," Connor said with a sigh.

"Bye, Connor, nice to meet you April, though I wish it could have been in much happier circumstances."

"Yeah, I feel the same."

As Judd climbed into the truck and drove away, Connor stood back and stared up at the entrance.

"What are you thinking?" April asked, looping her arm through his. "Are you having second thoughts about rebuilding?"

"Nope," he said firmly. "I'll take the insurance money and sell this piece of land to finance the ranch, but I want to take this frontage and put a small version of the tavern there."

"Because...?"

"Because, April," he murmured, turning to face her, "I want to keep my Thanksgiving tradition alive. It's when and where I met you."

* * *

April couldn't have been happier as they drove to the Sheriff's office. The intoxicating combination of Connor's confident authority and his sentimental soul made her toes curl and her heart sing. As he rolled to a stop near the front doors, she leaned across and kissed him on the cheek.

"What's that for?" he asked with a grin.

"Just because," she replied, then quickly kissed him again and climbed out. "I hope this will be over soon."

"Me too," Connor said, putting his arm around her shoulders as they walked to the entrance, "though I doubt it, but I'd like to forget about it all with a mug of my special hot chocolate, a blazing fire, and an old movie."

"That sounds perfect. You have the best ideas."

"Hardly, ideas are your department."

Moving through the doors and up to the reception area, Connor introduced himself to the deputy behind the counter and asked for the sheriff.

"I'll let him know you're here," the young man said, picking up his desk phone. "Sorry about your tavern, I'll miss that place."

"Thanks, it was a home away from home for a lot of people."

"It sure was for me," the deputy said earnestly. "You probably remember me as Derrick. I used to hog the jukebox."

"Derrick?" Connor exclaimed, staring at him intently. "Damn. I didn't recognize you without your cowboy hat."

"Sorry, excuse me for a second," he whispered. "Sheriff, Connor McBride is here. Yes, sir." Hanging up the receiver, he pointed to door marked STAFF ONLY. "Just go through there. The sheriff is the second on the left."

"Thanks, Derrick."

Opening the door and ushering April in ahead of him, he spotted Wes stepping into the hall.

"Hey, Connor," Wes said, waving them forward. "Come on in."

"Our statements are in here, along with the CD's with the security footage," Connor said, entering the comfortable office and handing him the envelope.

"Great, have a seat while I take a quick look," Wes said, opening the flap and pulling them out. "These look good, you put all the information exactly where it should be and signed it correctly. I'll read them through after you leave. If I need anything else I'll let you know, but before you leave, there are some things you should know about the Churchills."

"You mean you've spoken with them?" April asked, leaning forward in her chair. "What did they say?"

"Not in depth, I wanted to view the footage and read your statements, but you have a right to know what I'm about to tell you. A couple of years ago, three part-time workers were killed in a cabin on the Churchill Estate. Their deaths were ruled accidental, but I wasn't convinced," he said solemnly, then pausing dramatically, he added, "They were trapped in a fire."

"What the hell...?" Connor muttered.

"Needless to say, I'll be re-openin' that case, but there's more," the sheriff said gravely. "Last year, the night after thanksgivin', a young woman from out of town was the victim of a hit-and-run. It was the middle of the night, and it happened just a couple of miles from the Churchill Chateau."

"No..." April breathed, shaking her head as a chill pricked her skin. "Was she staying there?"

"I'm not sure. Her family said she'd been on a three week vacation traveling around this part of the country. She'd told them she'd met someone special. That was a few days before the incident. It's still an open case."

"This is horrible," April continued. "Could there be others?"

"That's what I'm wondering," Wes muttered grimly.

"Sheriff, I have to tell you, the Churchill wives, they're like robots. This might sound far-fetched, but is it possible they're drugged?"

"Or scared to death to put a foot wrong," Connor interjected.

"The thing is," April continued, her face crinkling at the memory, "at dinner there were always two pills sitting in front of their plates. Richard told me they were vitamins. He tried to persuade me to take them, but I told him I was already on a strict vitamin regimen through my doctor, which I am. Maybe they were sedatives. Those poor women seemed to be walking around in a daze."

"Damn," Connor exclaimed. "What the hell is goin' on in that place?"

"I'm about to find out," Wes said, his lips pursing with determination. "I'm expectin' the search warrant to arrive any minute now. I plan to bring everyone in that house to the station to be interviewed and fingerprinted. Maybe away from their men, these women will open up, and I've already ordered a couple of my deputies to start investigatin' missin' persons reports. Connor, it's thanks to your security cameras I can jump all over this. With irrefutable proof Richard Churchill blew up your tavern, I can turn that chateau upside down."

"Sheriff, where did the Churchill's come from?" April asked. "What's their history?"

"Henry moved here with a bunch of money, his wife and young sons from upstate New York years ago. That's all I know, but now I'll be diggin', and I'm sure in a few days I'll have a whole lot more to tell you," he declared as a knock sounded on his door. "Come in."

"This just arrived for you, Sheriff," a deputy said, walking in and handing him an envelope.

"Finally! The search warrant," Wes exclaimed, quickly pulling out the document. "Time to get to work."

"Sheriff, I have a favor to ask," April said as she and Connor rose to their feet. "When you go in, would it be possible to get my things? When I took off, all I grabbed was my bag and a coat. My suitcase and clothes are still there."

"I'll be happy to. Before you leave, write a description of the items and where your bedroom was located inside the chateau, and give it to the deputy at the front desk on your way out."

"Fantastic, thank you."

"I'll put you in an interview room and send someone in with a pad and paper, and April, thanks for tellin' me about those pills. I'll make sure my boys bring in everything they find, down to the last aspirin bottle. I've gotta feelin' the Churchill men will be sleepin' in my cells tonight."

"Uh, Sheriff," April said hastily, "what about the horses?"

"Good question, and that depends. If the Churchill's are remanded, the animal welfare folks will be called."

"I'd like to make a suggestion," she said earnestly, looking up at Connor. "I know you only have four stalls, but what about your neighbor's barn? There's plenty of room there, and you said it was in good condition."

"It sure is," Connor exclaimed, a surge of excitement moving through his body. "Wes, if it comes to that, I'm sure I can work out an arrangement, and I'll definitely be open to adopting them if that's where things end up."

"That sure would save the folks at the shelter a lotta time and trouble. I'll let you know."

"See, April, I told you," Connor whispered as Wes led them down the hall to an interview room, "you're the one with the great ideas."

"Here you go," Wes declared, opening a door. "Make yourselves at home. One of my boys will be in soon, and I'll make sure they bring you in some coffee."

"Thanks for everything," April said gratefully. "I didn't think I'd ever see my things again."

"Glad I could help. I'll see you two later."

"As I was saying," Connor continued as the sheriff left and closed the door behind him, "that suggestion was genius."

"I have my moments."

"You sure do, and while you're makin' that list, I'm callin' Bill," Connor declared, pulling his phone from his pocket.

"Bill?"

"My neighbor. I'd better make sure I haven't jumped the gun, but he did tell me he couldn't wait to see his property put to good use."

"I hope it all works out. You could end up with some really nice horses."

Placing his arm around her shoulders, he leaned in and placed his lips at her ear.

"If that happens, I promise you're in for a very special thank you..."

CHAPTER FOURTEEN

With his neighbor's enthusiastic blessing, and knowing the twelve-stall barn needed cleaning out, Connor placed a call to Lance on the drive home.

"Hey, Connor," Lance said, answering on the first ring. "What's up?"

"A lot, too much to explain now, but I'm pretty sure I'll be takin' in the horses from the Churchill estate."

"How many are there?"

"Ten."

"Lord, Connor, where will you put them?"

"That's why I'm callin'. I'm buyin' that property next door, and the owner's agreed to let me put them there."

"That's great."

"Yeah, but I need to be ready. Can you spare those three ranch hands of yours tomorrow to help me clean it up?"

"You bet, and I'll join them," Lance replied enthusiastically. "Do you need a truckload of hay to tide you over?"

"Thanks, but if it happens, the feed will be brought over from the Churchill's. These horses are bound to be on all kinds of supplements. I just hope everything is clearly marked."

"It is," April interjected. "That barn is very organized."

"Connor, how can you be so sure this will happen?" Lance asked. "The Churchills could be charged and released on bail."

"It's possible, but I doubt it. You know Judge Turley. He won't let anyone out if there's even the slightest chance they could bolt. It's the wives and children I'm worried about. April said they walked around like zombies. She's sure they were drugged."

"If that's the case, they'll be taken to the hospital, and there's a women's shelter over in Haywood, but Wes will figure it out. As far as tomorrow goes, we'll be there around eight. How does that sound?"

"That sounds great. Thanks, Lance."

"You're welcome. I'll see you then."

"I take it they're coming?" April remarked as Connor ended the call and turned through the gates of his home.

"Yep, Lance and his boys will be here first thing."

Following the driveway past the garage to the back of the house, he continued to the barn. Mitch and Molly were in their small paddock, and whinnied loudly as the Jeep approached.

"They'll be so excited to see a new herd," April said with a grin. "I hope it's not too much for them."

"Are you kiddin'? They'll love it."

Coming to a stop and stepping out, they paused to pet the two happy horses, then opened the gate and walked the short distance to the neighboring facility.

"It's not as bad as I thought," Connor declared, walking down the aisle and poking his head in the stalls.

"This tack room has everything you need," April declared, staring into the dusty space. "Saddle and bridle racks, cupboards and shelving. It's perfect. Do you think Suzy will help me clean it up?"

"I was just about to call her. She'll be thrilled about this" he replied, reaching for his phone. "Looks like I'm gonna have a ranch on my hands sooner than I thought. I know Bill's happy to let me use it, but now I wanna firm up the deal."

"Speaking as a lawyer's daughter, with everything that's happening, you should," April said solemnly, "and I bet he's just as eager as you are to get things settled."

* * *

The remainder of the afternoon sailed by. While Connor negotiated the purchase of his neighbor's property in his office, April sat in the living room in front of the fire using Connor's laptop to search out deals for the supplies they'd need.

"Hey, April, I've got a problem," Connor declared, startling her as he suddenly marched into the room. "Bill and I have a deal, but my lawyer is gone until after the first of the year and I need something in writing."

April broke into a wide smile.

"No problem, I can draft a Memorandum of Understanding. Just give me the details."

"Seriously? You know how to do that?"

"Sure, but when I'm done I'll read it through with dad just to make sure I have it right. You'll be able to drop it off tonight. What's your neighbor's name?"

"Bill Meyers. William J. Meyers to be exact."

She caught her breath.

"*The* William J. Meyers?" she asked, staring up at Connor with wide eyes.

"Uh...I don't know. Who is *the* William J. Meyers?"

"Only one of the most renowned three-day eventers in the country."

"Then I guess that's the guy. I've seen him jumping around his arena."

"Uh, Connor..." April began hesitantly, then pausing, she muttered, "I'm not sure how to tell you this."

"Just spit it out," he said, sitting next to her.

"Something just occurred to me, and uh..."

"Now you're startin' to worry me. What is it?"

"Did you know the Churchill's horses are jumpers and high level dressage."

"Holy crap!"

"Jumping is my passion, but I'm not sure I'd be able to handle those beauties."

"I'm not about to back out now," he declared. "I'll just have to figure out how to deal with it."

"I think I already have buyers for two of them. Does that help?"

"Yeah," he replied with a grin. "It does, a lot!"

She paused, a slight frown creasing her brow.

"What is it?" he asked, "I can almost see your brain workin.'"

"I have an idea..."

"I'll just bet you do," he said, laughing out loud. "Write the memo. I'll let Lance know, then I'll start dinner. You can tell me all about it while we eat."

"Sounds like a plan."

Giving her a quick peck on the cheek, he rose to his feet and headed out the door. April heard his phone ring, but she was already focused on finding the right form online. It didn't take her long to make the necessary adjustments and mail it to her father, along with a quick explanation of the situation. He shot it back to her with only minor changes, and a note saying she should still think about law as a career. Smiling as she read it, she had just finished making the corrections when Connor burst back into the room.

"April! I've been talking to Wes."

"All this time?" she asked as he hurried over and sat next to her.

"You won't believe what he just told me," Connor continued urgently. "I don't even know where to start."

"Start where he did."

"Yeah, right, good idea. Edward is gay. He hates his father and brothers, and he spilled his guts."

"You're kidding," she exclaimed, staring at him.

"He said he kept trying to get your attention. That's why he was staring. He wanted to warn you, not scare you."

"Oh, my gosh."

"But there's so much more. Henry Churchill's real name is Harry Chapman, and he didn't come from back east. He's from Southern California. He's wanted in connection with the death of his wife. She was found strangled in the basement of their home, and Edward swears his father killed her."

"Good grief."

"Guess how Henry, or rather, Harry, made his money in L.A. Are you ready?"

"Yes, yes, tell me!"

"Narcotics. He was a drug dealer. Apparently he left so much evidence behind it was obvious he'd taken off in a hurry. Anyway, Edward told him where to look, and during the search of the chateau, Wes found all kinds of pharmaceuticals. Henry, or rather Harry, controlled the women and children with a variety of drugs. They're in the hospital now."

"That's horrible, but thank goodness they're getting the care they need, but Connor, can you imagine the stories they'll be able to tell? When you said we'd opened a hornet's nest, you weren't kidding."

"Edward's been desperate to get away, but he was too terrified to try. His brothers and father have no idea he's gay, and they were insisting it was time for him to take a wife."

"So...what happens now?"

"For starters, the Churchills are facin' a laundry list of charges. They're not goin' anywhere. I'm not sure about Edward though. Wes said it appears he's almost as much a victim as the women."

"Did Wes say anything about the horses?"

"Yep, and it's great news. Animal Welfare are arrangin' a van to transport them here, along with the hay and all their stuff. We need to have the stalls ready by three o'clock tomorrow afternoon."

"I'm sure we can do that," she said confidently, "although...won't the horses belong to Edward if he's cleared?"

"Edward's legal situation is up in the air, but regardless, the chateau and its contents will be seized, including the livestock, but horses can't be taken to a warehouse and locked away. Wes said Animal Welfare are grateful they'll be taken off their hands. I'll be considered a foster home until the adoption papers are drawn up, which should only take a couple of weeks, then I'll pay the fees and they'll be mine."

"Connor, this is the best news ever," April exclaimed, throwing her arms around his neck.

"All because you walked into my tavern," he murmured, dropping his voice as he wrapped her up. "April, when you sat on that barstool and downed that beer, you damn near gave me a heart attack," he continued, pulling back and cupping her chin. "I know you live hours away, and we've been caught up in a crazy, scary, wild ride that's thrown us together, but I swear, darlin', I want you in my life. Can we work this out? Do you want to?"

"Of course we can and of course I do," she mumbled, trying to control the threat of happy tears. "I don't have to go back for at least a couple of weeks. I'm not about to leave you in the lurch with those horses. You need my help."

"You're right about that," he said with a grin, then sliding his fingers into her hair, he leaned in and glided his lips over hers.

As he swept her away in an endless, languid, loving kiss, she felt herself turning into mush. When he finally brought it to an end, breathless and happy, she sank against his body.

* * *

Closing his eyes and relishing the feel of her, Connor held April in his arms until the chiming of the antique clock on the mantle broke the spell.

"I guess we should deliver that memo to Bill," he muttered, slowly pulling back.

"You need to read it before you sign it and take it over, but what kind of guy is he? Do you know why he retired?"

"He's easy goin', friendly, and yeah, I do. After his wife died he lost his drive to compete, so he decided it was time to slip away somewhere quiet and pursue his other passion, oil paintin'. He's really talented. His work is mostly horse related. I even bought one. It's in the hall."

"Connor, remember I said I had an idea?"

"Yeah?" he replied with a chuckle. "Go ahead, what's rattlin' around that brilliant brain of yours?"

"I can help you market the horses, but not like Bill Meyer. He's highly respected and a big name. He'll know all kinds of people. I think you should offer him a percentage to make some calls. It's worth a try."

"Damn, that's a great suggestion. He's had family with him, but they've left. Workin' on this might help fill the void. Let's go talk to him."

"Wait, there's more."

"Why aren't I surprised? Go on."

"Unless I'm missing something, you're not a trainer. If you want to have a training facility you'll have to bring someone in, and—"

"I'm gonna stop you right there," he said, interrupting her. "Lance and I have talked about this. I don't have the experience to open any kind of trainin' or breedin' facility. All I can offer at this point is boardin', and that's fine. I just want a barn full of horses and a bunch of dogs runnin' around."

"Great! So—how would you feel about bringing in more horses like Mitch and Molly? It's really hard to find decent retirement homes, and you won't have to deal with a bunch of people coming and going all the time."

"April, I love that idea," he exclaimed. "There's somethin' special about bein' around those two old souls."

"You should have a graphic of a horse wearing glasses, smoking a pipe, and sitting in an armchair reading the paper."

"Hah, another brilliant suggestion, and maybe Bill will even paint it for me. Seems like things are fallin' into place."

"Assuming Bill's up for it."

"He will be," Connor said confidently.

"How can you be so sure?"

"Did you forget that magical moon?" he said softly, leaning in and planting a soft kiss on her mouth. "You, me, this ranch, it's all meant to be."

EPILOGUE

As Connor predicted, Bill Meyer responded enthusiastically when asked if he'd be interested in helping with the sale of the horses.

"We need to give them a few days to settle in and make sure any drugs are out of their system, and I'll call in my niece. She's on the circuit but things are quiet this time of year. She can come down for a few days and put them through their paces with me. Once we know what we've got on our hands, I'll know who to contact. If they're as nice as you say, I suggest hosting a weekend event. I'll invite a few trainers and riders. They can fight over the goods."

"Do you think they will?" Connor asked. "Fight I mean?"

"It can happen. There's bound to be a couple of standouts. I suggest sealed bids."

As the conversation continued, Connor noticed April was unusually quiet. Even when Bill signed the memo, she seemed preoccupied. The sun had set by the time they left, and walking through the cold night back to the house, Connor put his arm around her shoulders.

"Are you gonna tell me what's wrong?"

"Wrong?" she repeated, darting her eyes up.

"Maybe I can help."

"I didn't realize I was that transparent," she mumbled, letting out a sigh.

"Maybe you're not. Maybe I can just pick up on what you're feelin'. Tell me, darlin', what's botherin' you?"

Taking a long, breath, she shook her head and leaned against him.

"I committed the cardinal sin," she began softly. "I bonded with one of the horses. She's only sixteen hands. Henry asked me to ride her because his boys are tall and lanky and he wanted to see her with a rider my size. She's a dream, and she's so sweet. I swear she wanted to crawl into my lap. I'd love it if she could stay in your barn until she's sold, but then it will break my heart even more when she goes. It's probably better I don't see her at all."

"April, why didn't you tell me this before. She doesn't have to go anywhere."

"What do you mean?"

"You know what I mean," he murmured, taking her gloved hands. "I don't know why there's no horse in your life right now, but you need one. It's who you are."

"My thoroughbred...I lost her a few months ago. I've been so busy I just haven't had the time to look. That's not true," she suddenly admitted. "I haven't had it in me."

"But now you've met Bonny, and she's special, right?"

"Even more than I thought. I've been so worried about her, but—"

"But what? Don't you want her?"

"I do," she whispered, "very much, but she's part of the—"

"She's part of us. It's settled," he said firmly. "When the adoption papers come through, Bonny is yours."

"Oh, my gosh," April said breathlessly, happy tears springing from her eyes as she hugged him. "Thank you so much."

"No, April, thank you," he managed, fighting his own swell of emotion.

"For what?" she asked, pulling back and staring up at him.

"Lettin' me into your great big heart."

* * *

New Year's Eve

* * *

For the first time since arriving in the sleepy town, Connor hosted a New Year's party. Lance and Annabelle had found a baby-sitter and arrived with plates of food, and Bill Meyer had a surprise guest on his arm. During the sale of the horses, he'd reconnected with a trainer named Suzanne. Wes and his wife had stopped in, as did many others who were once regulars at the tavern.

As the clock struck midnight, and the party wound down, Connor and April stood at the door waving goodbye to the last of the guests.

"What an amazing holiday," she exclaimed, leaning wearily against Connor as they moved back inside. "Exhausting but amazing. I'm so glad we decided to take the plunge."

"You were the one who made it happen. You can be a very determined woman when you want to be."

"It was our first Christmas, and we have so much to celebrate going into the New Year. The Churchill's are out of business for a long time, and—"

"They're outta business for good," Connor said vehemently, interrupting her, "especially now the wives are out of their stupor and talkin'."

"Those poor women, but at least they're free and reunited with their families."

"Yep, and we found great homes for the horses and made a packet. Once the sale is finalized, we can really make that retirement facility something special."

"I wish I didn't have to leave," she mumbled as they made their way into the kitchen. "I know it's only for a week, but I'll miss you and Bonny so much."

"About that..." he said softly.

"What?"

"I'm comin' with you. I need to meet your parents. I've already booked a hotel."

"Why didn't you say anything?"

"I've been waitin' for the right moment," he said softly, taking her hands. "We belong together, and I don't wanna waste any time, so, uh,

I'll be askin' your dad for his blessin'. What I'm tryin' to say is, April, will you spend the rest of your life with me? Will you marry me?"

"Oh, my gosh, of course I—"

Before she could finish, he lifted her up and spun her around, eliciting a loud squeal, but as he stood her back down his face grew serious.

"I love you with everything in me, darlin'."

Planting his lips on hers in a crushing, passionate kiss, she melted in his arms, sure her heart would burst with joy.

"Now I'm gonna seal the deal with a New Year's spankin'," he declared, abruptly pulling back and lifting her off her feet.

Carrying her up the stairs and into the bedroom, he tossed her on the bed, made quick work of removing her clothes, then hurriedly stripped.

"Lay over my lap," he ordered, climbing on the bed and resting his back against the padded headboard.

As she crawled over his muscled thighs, he roamed his hands over her backside, occasionally slipping his fingers into her sex, but waiting until she was wriggling with anticipation before delivering the first few slaps. Slowly increasing the force, when her squirms and an occasional kick told him her bottom was becoming tender, he returned his attention to her pussy and pushed his finger into her slick channel.

"That feels so good," she purred as he shoved it in and out. "Please, don't stop."

Grinning a wicked grin, he withdrew his hand, evoking a disappointed groan. Sliding his palm back across her blushing behind, he landed a flurry of hot smacks, then quickly returned his fingers to fervently massage her clit.

"Please, please," she gasped, wriggling furiously as she pleaded.

"Please what?"

"Please can I come?"

"Not quite yet," he replied, slowing his fingers. "Your ass is so red."

"It feels like it," she squeaked. "It's hot, it's hot like me."

"Slide off my lap and get on to your hands and knees."

As she crawled into position, he donned a condom, then kneeled behind her and held himself at her entrance.

"You ready, darlin'?"

"Yes, yes, please."

Gripping her hips, he thrust inside her, continuing to pump with strong, quick strokes.

* * *

Her backside tingling with a delicious prickling heat, and Connor's hard cock pounding her pussy, April's orgasm threatened to break at any moment. But every time she reached the crest of the mighty wave, he would slow down, or stop altogether. Now pumping her with slow, deliberate strokes, unable to wait a second longer, she threw her hand between her legs to rub her clit.

"Ask permission," he growled, quickly grabbing her wrist.

"Please, Connor," she wailed, "I'm desperate to come. Please..."

"Yeah, darlin, you can come."

The husky promise had almost been enough to send her over the edge. As he released her to clutch her hip, she gasped out her gratitude and began the erotic massage.

Sparkling sensations hovered.

He'd been slowly thrusting, but suddenly accelerating, she had to drop her hand back to the mattress to keep her balance. Feeling the powerful climax about to burst, she held her breath...

Brilliant lights flashed through her brain as wave after scintillating wave sent quivering tingles down her limbs. Though she could hear his groans, her squeals of pleasure drowned them out, until the last convulsion shuddered through her body, leaving her panting and breathless as she collapsed on her stomach.

She felt him flop next to her.

Managing to slide closer, she snuggled in to him and rested her head on his chest. His heart thumped heavy against her ear. Letting out a heavy breath, the drumbeat stayed with her as she drifted...

* * *

"Best Christmas and New Year's ever," Connor murmured as he emerged from the serene haze.

"Ever," April repeated. "It was one miracle after another."

"What's the first order of business when we get back?"

"Uh, I'm not sure, but assume you're about to tell me."

"A visit to the animal shelter," he declared. "We need some dogs around this place. I had planned on gettin' a couple for Christmas as a surprise, but I knew I'd be takin' off for a few days to meet your parents."

"What kind do you want?"

"Four legs, a wet nose, and a tail."

"I love that breed," she exclaimed, laughing out loud, then propping herself up on an elbow, she stared down at him. "I'm glad you waited. It's something we should do together."

"Yep, I thought about that too. April, is there anything else you want? Anything that would make these holidays even better?"

Letting out a heavy sigh, she climbed on top of him, placed her hands on either side of his head, and lingered her lips over his.

"When I walked into the tavern and saw you behind the bar," she murmured, breaking the kiss and gazing down at him, "I said to myself, *That's what I want for Christmas, that sexy, hunky cowboy.* I still can't quite believe my wish came true. Connor, there's nothing else I need or want, you're my everything. You're my Christmas cowboy, and you always will be."

Dear Reader:

Thank you for buying this book. If you have a moment I would greatly appreciate your review. I constantly strive to bring readers interesting and enjoyable content and your feedback is valued. Feel free to contact me at MagCarpenter@yahoo.com, and my social media links are listed below.

My very best wishes,

Maggie

https://www.MaggieCarpenter.com
https://www.facebook.com/MaggieCarpenterWriter

BOOKS BY MAGGIE CARPENTER

#1 Bestseller
ROUGH COWBOY

* * *

HUNKS and HORSES
A FOUR BOOK SERIES - HEA - STANDALONE
(Featuring characters from COWBOY: His Ranch. His Rules. His Secrets)
TO KISS A COWBOY
TO CATCH A COWBOY
TO CON A COWBOY
TO TRUST A COWBOY

* * *

SEXY SCIFI - PARANORMAL
ROUGH ALPHA
TRAINED BY THE ALIEN
WARLOCK
THE ALIEN'S RULES

* * *

BDSM CONTEMPORARY ROMANCE
FIFTY SHADES OF SPY
ROUGH ROAD
ROUGH ROCKSTAR
THE STRICT BRITISH BARRISTER: BOOKS 1 & 2
SINS BEHIND THE SCENES
I AM A DOMINANT
DESIRE UNLEASHED - Sexsomnia
TIMELESS OBSESSION

* * *

For a full list of her novels visit her author page.
https://www.amazon.com/author/maggiecarpente

www.ingramcontent.com/pod-product-compliance
Lightning Source LLC
Chambersburg PA
CBHW021118130626
46554CB00002B/757